With his eyes closed, ~~~~ ~~~~~~~~~~~ could see even more clearly the glorified face of the girl who had looked up at him in adoring surrender. He knew that he wanted her for his wife above anything else the world could hold.

But she was still a child, her devotion innocent of all trace of passion. She loved him because she saw him as the very figure of romance. There was no reality in such love. It was the stuff that dreams were made of and would never survive the touch of harsh reality.

If he guarded her carefully, left her free to grow into a woman, and wooed her delicately the while, might it not be that she would learn to love him as he so deeply desired? Not as a dream prince, but as a man—warm—faulty—human...

LISSA

a novel by

MIRA STABLES

FAWCETT CREST • NEW YORK

LISSA

THIS BOOK CONTAINS THE COMPLETE TEXT OF THE
ORIGINAL HARDCOVER EDITION.

Published by Fawcett Crest Books, a unit of CBS Publications, the
Consumer Publishing Division of CBS Inc., by arrangement with
Robert Hale Limited

Copyright © 1974 by Mira Stables
ALL RIGHTS RESERVED

ISBN: 0-449-24138-6

Selection of the Doubleday Romance Library

Printed in the United States of America

10 9 8 7 6 5 4 3 2 1

For
Alexa, Jessica, and Mira Joanne

Chapter 1

"YOUR WILD extravagance, your reckless risk of life and limb in every crazy start that your so-called friends can invent for their entertainment, even your dangerous dabbling in the muddy waters of dubious political philosophy I have tolerated, in the belief that sooner or later your blood and breeding must bring you to your senses. You are not, after all, the first young idiot who has raised riot and rumpus the moment that he was thrown on the Town. But this time you have gone your length. It is not so much your ridiculous politics—though I may say in passing that it is only thanks to my intervention that you are not facing trial for seditious utterances—as the fact that you have made a laughing stock of yourself and of our family name. We have numbered some consummate villains among our ancestors but I cannot call to mind a single one so simple as to have fallen to such a man-trap—such an obvious man-trap as seems to have be-glamoured you out of your senses. A pair of bold black eyes, red lips and

honey-sweet words—and a heart more greedy for
gold than Judas Iscariot's. And you to dream of
marrying the strumpet! Why! I tell you her favours
have been for sale to the highest bidder, so he be
wealthy and discreet, any time these past five
years. Young Hartdale was the last fool she
cozened before she set her dainty little claws in
you, and a pretty penny it cost his father to be rid of
her. And you, *my* grandson, must needs season
your puling love letters to the doxy with sickly
maunderings about the wonderful re-birth of
liberty and equality across the Channel. As
though the price of your green-sickness were not
high enough, you furnish her with proof of your
treasonable beliefs. I suppose it has escaped your
notice that we are at war with those very
blood-swilling rascals that you praise so high.
There are your letters, though God alone knows
why I should be at such pains to save your silly
neck. Burn them, now, and make an end."

A wooden image might have shown more
reaction to the scathing tirade, he thought bitterly,
watching Jervase pick up the bundle of letters in
which he had poured out a young man's dreams of
a noble and rapturous future spent with the
woman whom he had believed to be as pure souled
and high minded as she was beautiful. Almost
absently he dropped them into the library fire and
stood watching them shrivel to ashes as dead and
grey and useless as his dreams. As the brief glow
died away he turned quietly back to face the old
autocrat who had sheltered his boyhood and
guided his youth and then, in default of the Grand

Tour which had completed the wordly education of the boy's father, which the present European ferment rendered ineligible, had thrown him upon the Town with complete freedom and ample resources to satisfy his smallest whim.

The Marquis of Wrelf could see no fault in his own conduct. The boy had enjoyed every advantage that wealth could provide. He had been given a sound classical education and had enjoyed his time at Oxford even if it was distinguished more by sporting achievements than by academic brilliance. And, indeed, apart from the shattering débâcle of his first love affair, the Marquis was not ill-pleased with the way his heir was shaping. He was a first-rate swordsman and a useful shot, while the horse was not yet foaled that he could not master. A little recklessness was allowable, even desirable, in hot, young blood. He was generally well-liked, did not gamble more than was socially desirable and his cronies were a lively set of wild young scamps who shared his sporting tastes. Why then this inexplicable streak of maudlin sentiment? My lord was much inclined to lay the blame on the boy's long-dead mother. Impeccably bred and educated as she had, of course, been, since he himself had selected her for her exalted role, *she* had nurtured an odd taste for poetry had even gone so far as to write the stuff herself. His lordship, who had no patience with such effeminate stuff, wondered if it was this poetic streak that was showing itself in her son. Certainly those letters—! He pressed a fine linen handkerchief to his lips. He had been obliged to scan them—not being such a simpleton as to pay handsomely without inspecting the goods he bought.

Since the culprit seemed to have nothing to say for himself, the Marquis resumed the attack. "It is clearly necessary that you leave Town until the scandal has had time to die," he said austerely. "You will betake yourself to Wrelf or to Stapleford, whichever you prefer, and concern yourself with the care of our estates until such time as some bigger fool becomes the target for Society's sly whispers and raised eyebrows."

For the first time there came a hint of animation into Lord Stapleford's rigid face. "With your permission, my lord, I would rather journey overseas. I have long wished to travel in the Americas and this would seem to be my opportunity."

Despite his present justifiable anger the Marquis had no desire to expose his heir to the unknown dangers that such a journey might hold. Apart from shipwreck, plague and violence and such other hazards as were commonplace in any journey abroad, he was being asked to accept the boy's sojourn among a pack of pesky rebels, traitors to their king, men who had had the infernal impudence to defeat Britain's might and to compel the surrender of whole armies in the field. Moreover he would be subjected to the attentions of as treacherous and bloodthirsty a native populace as ever sharpened tomahawks. No one would ever convince the Marquis that his notions of the Americas were distinctly biased, but he knew that a warning of possible danger would be no deterrent. He must be a little devious.

"So you are a poltroon, as well as a simpleton," he said softly, more in resignation than in anger.

That was better. The boy's head came up with a snap, the dark eyes flashed fiercely. But he spoke gently enough. "No other man has ever called me so, my lord. Your age and our close relationship give you leave."

"But do not excuse my insolence, eh? Very well, my boy. Your point is taken. Now, tell me. How else would you describe one who, when under something of a cloud, chooses to—er—travel abroad, leaving an aged relative to endure as best he may the sniggers and the innuendoes which he is too feeble openly to resent?"

He had overplayed his hand. Jervase grinned. "As to that, Sir," he riposted, formality going by the board, "you would be reaching for your sword hilt before the first word was even breathed. However, I will forgive you for 'poltroon' and will confess myself, if not yet exactly grateful, at least much obliged to you. If it will please you better I will consent to retire to one of our rural fastnesses to sit out my exile. Which one shall it be?"

The old man shrugged. "As you wish. It is a matter of indifference to me."

"Then I shall choose Stapleford and bear Mary company for a while. Wrelf is too familiar. It would be all too easy to slide into a melancholy there," he pronounced mockingly. "And that, I take it, is no part of your plans for curing me of my youthful folly. No, do not protest, Sir. I know you too well, you see. Tell me what you have in mind for my ultimate reformation."

The Marquis's scowl relaxed a little and the keen grey eyes gleamed approbation. There was even the hint of a wry smile tugging at the corner of his mouth as he replied coolly, "Since you choose Stapleford, you may make yourself useful. Pursey must soon retire—indeed he is long past active service—but his head is stuffed with invaluable knowledge about the place and the tenantry. You will do well to learn of him and you may deal with any slackness that his infirmities have permitted to creep in."

His grandson bowed politely. "An enlivening prospect," he said gravely. "Would it be troubling you too far to ask for the truth?"

The Marquis had never been famous for his control over a quick temper that combined ill with his masterful disposition. "Certainly you shall hear," he snapped. "Not to wrap it up in clean linen, it's time you had more experience with women, Stapleford. You were never one for the petticoats, and I've been glad of it, until you showed me how easily such innocence is brought to disaster. Had your knowledge of the sex been wider, you had never fallen for the cheap charms of Millicent Girling. Go down to Stapleford. Seduce some village wench—or half a dozen if that is more to your taste. These little affairs are understood in the country. The wenches are willing enough so long as you provide for them generously, and in Stapleford you will need some form of entertainment. The society of your sister will scarcely suffice to beguile your boredom. Go and learn about women, boy, before you again think of marriage."

Viscount Stapleford met his grandsire's eyes levelly. His expression was calm, almost bland. He said, "I will so far accede to your wishes, my lord, as to betake myself to Stapleford and turn diligent apprentice to Pursey. For the rest—permit me to inform your lordship that for the first time in our acquaintance I find you shockingly ill-bred."

Without waiting for any reply from the fulminating Marquis, he bowed again and went swiftly from the room.

Chapter 2

MRS. WAYBURN bustled about cheerfully, setting her pleasant kitchen to rights. A sense of pleased anticipation informed her movements. She always looked forward to Thursdays when she went up to the Place to sew. Mrs. Graham, the housekeeper, was her closest friend, and the two of them would enjoy a comfortable cose while Annie Wayburn set her fine stitches in such articles of household linen as stood in need of attention. They were never very many. Stapleford Place was rarely visited by its noble owner, who seemed to prefer the magnificence of Wrelf with its endless facilities for sport of every kind. Only the Lady Mary, with her governess resided permanently at Stapleford, the air of Wrelf not suiting her delicate constitution.

But from what Mrs. Wayburn had heard this state of affairs would soon be changed. Not the Marquis himself but young Viscount Stapleford was expected, and, it was understood, for a prolonged stay. This afternoon she would hear all about it. It would be good to have another of the family in residence. Bring a bit of life about the place. She gathered up her sewing basket, cast a final glance at the smouldering fire to see that all was safe, and then clicked her teeth in annoyance at the sound of a rather hesitating knock. Who could be wanting her at such an inconvenient hour? Everyone knew that she went out on Thursday.

Perhaps this importunate visitor did indeed know and wanted to be assured that she had not already left home, for next the latch was tried and then the door itself opened a little way to allow a head to peep round it. "Lizzie!" exclaimed Mrs. Wayburn, surprise and pleasure in her voice, and then, more doubtfully, "But what are you doing here?"

The caller now seemed to take courage to come into the kitchen, and it was seen that she was carrying a large straw basket, a basket which was only too familiar to Mrs. Wayburn. An expression of dismay appeared on her plump and kindly countenance. "Never say you've been turned off?" she said sharply.

Her visitor nodded, put down the basket, and ran to throw warm young arms about her ample waist in an affectionate hug, saying as she kissed her, "Yes, I have. Don't be cross, Nanty. Indeed it was not entirely my fault—well scarcely at all, really—and anyway I hated it and am glad to have done with it."

"That's as may be," declared Mrs. Wayburn, trying to harden her heart against the child. "But good places don't grow on every bush and you know very well that you've your own way to make in the world now that the money's stopped coming. And on a Thursday, too, when I can't stay to hear the full tale. You know it's my sewing afternoon."

The girl's face filled with wistful longing. "Can't I come with you, Nanty? It's ages since I've been up to the Place. Perhaps Mrs. Graham will let me look at the pictures."

Mrs. Wayburn hesitated. But a desire to hear as soon as possible how her fosterling had come to lose a desirable post worked strongly in the culprit's favour and she gave consent. The girl could be sent to amuse herself in wandering about the great silent rooms and galleries as she loved to do if she and Aggie wanted to talk secrets.

They set out at once, the girl carrying the sewing basket and pouring out the tale of the misadventure that had procured her dismissal. "Truly it was Bertha's own fault, though both she and Mrs. Williams said I'd done it on purpose. I think Bertha really hates me. She was jealous when the Vicar offered to give me lessons after I was done with school and didn't ask her to come too. I'm sure she persuaded her mother to employ me just so that she could order me about and get her own back. You've no notion how spiteful she was, forever pinching and slapping me and knowing very well I couldn't slap back. And though I was supposed to be a sewing maid I had to wait on her and help her to dress and even put on her shoes and stockings as though she was a fine lady. Nothing I did was ever right. It was all grumbling and scolding. And then she started about my eyebrows."

Mrs. Wayburn looked puzzled, as well she might. "What's wrong with your eyebrows, lovey?"

"It was because they were dark. Bertha said I must have dyed them, because everybody knew that redheads always had white eyebrows and eyelashes. She wanted to know what I used. It seems she'd heard somewhere that dark beauties are all the crack, and you know how fair *she* is. She kept on and on about it until there was no bearing it and so at last I said that if I wanted to dye *my* hair—and goodness knows I often *did* want to when I was small—I'd use walnut oil. Well, she bought some and tried it on her eyebrows and was so pleased with the result that she went and got lots more and tried to dye her hair as well." An irrepressible chuckle bubbled up. "I wish you could have seen her, Nanty. She'd shut herself up in her room all day to do it, because her very best beau was coming to take her to the Fair and then when he called for her she wouldn't come down. The oil had made brown streaks all over her face and neck where it had trickled down and her hair looked more green than brown. Mrs. Williams was furious because she favours the match with Bob Shorthouse who owns his own farm and now he's taken the huff because Bertha wouldn't go to the Fair with him after he'd put himself to the trouble of driving over for her. Of course they couldn't tell him the real reason and nothing they've tried will take the dye out. So then Mrs. Williams said it was all my fault. Bertha would never have thought of doing such a thing if I hadn't put her up to it and

she wouldn't have me in the house any longer."
She stopped, the mischievous laughter fading
from face and voice as she went on slowly, "She
said a lot more things, too. About my parents. And
about bad blood coming out."

Mrs. Wayburn squeezed her hand in silent
sympathy. There was nothing she could say to
comfort. The child's birth was as much a mystery
now as it had been on the day that she had first
been brought to the cottage, a mischievous three-
year-old with red-gold curls and big grey eyes and
and an imperious way with her that betrayed her
breeding as clearly as did the sweet pure little voice
that insisted that her name was Lissa. Mrs.
Wayburn had taken that to be Elizabeth. The little
girl presently accepted the shortening of this name
to Lizzie and soon picked up the slow rustic speech
of the other children. Her looks marked her out as
different, of course. Slender and finely boned she
looked like a thoroughbred, thought Nanty, as the
child called her, this being her version of Auntie
Annie. Nanty sometimes grumbled that for all the
good food she gave her the child looked half
starved beside the sturdiness of her playmates.
Money had come regularly for her keep and there
had also been occasional surprise presents. Once
an exquisitely dressed doll had arrived—French,
Nanty reckoned—and a pretty penny it must have
cost. There had been a necklace of seed pearls, too,
and a beautifully bound prayer book. Surely
someone loved the little girl, someone of wealth
and good taste. Nanty was inclined to think that it
must be her mother. A man would scarcely have

thought of the doll. Privately she suspected that the child was the result of some secret liaison between two persons of quality rather than the infant born to a female in humble circumstances who had allowed herself to succumb to the wiles of an accomplished rake. Nanty had been brought up in good service until she had married her sailor and she knew the ways and looks of the quality when she saw them. There was no base blood in the child she was prepared to swear and she had done her best to bring her up properly. There had been money enough to pay for the dame school and then the Vicar and his wife had taken a hand, childless themselves and pitying the little one's forlorn condition. There had even been a tentative suggestion of sending her to one of the charity schools so that she might receive an education that would fit her for a post as a governess, but this had been scotched by the lawyer who had first placed the child with Nanty and who sent the money each month. If needful, money would be provided to send her to a respectable seminary at the proper time.

And then the payments had suddenly stopped; no warning, no message of explanation; just stopped. The lawyer could tell them no more. He suggested that his client might have fallen on hard times—might even be dead. Nanty was a widow. She owned the cottage in which she lived and she could find plenty of sewing work. But it was poorly paid. She could not afford to support a grown girl in idleness. To be sure she had been frugal. She had put by a nice little sum during the years when the

money had arrived regularly. But that was
intended for the time when her darling should
wish to marry. She had come to love her foster
child as dearly as she might have loved her own,
had she been so blessed. There might be difficulties
to be faced in marrying off a girl of unknown
parentage, even if she were pretty which Nanty
could not honestly say that she was, difficulties
which a dowry might smooth over. So the money
must not be touched and a respectable post must be
found. She had welcomed the offer of employment
at the Williams's farm as sewing maid. The
Williams family was respectable, Lizzie would be
well looked after and would have the company of
her old schoolmate, and as Bertha was an only
child there would be no young men to complicate
the situation. So she had thought in her own
natural kindliness. And now it was all to do again.
Perhaps Aggie Graham would be able to suggest
some post that would suit Lizzie. Such things were
often settled by a good recommendation from one
in Aggie's position. She relaxed and decided to
make the most of Lizzie's company while she had
it. The cottage had seemed a lonely place, lacking
that bright young presence.

Arrived in the housekeeper's sanctum, her
companion's presence explained and duly exclaimed over, Nanty settled herself comfortably to
the business of the afternoon. As her needle
flashed deftly in and out of the thin places in a
linen sheet she listened avidly to Aggie's account
of the arrival of his lordship. "Not so much as a
valet in attendance. Just his groom. And little to

say, though he smiles pleasant enough. And Mr.
Pursey quite overcome because his lordship is
willing to learn of him. But I sair misdoot the
outcome." In moments of emotion Agnes Graham
was apt to revert to her childhood accent. And she
was ever a prophet of gloom.

"Why, what ails him?" asked Mrs. Wayburn,
deeply interested.

"We don't know why he's come down here,"
began her friend, primming her lips severely, "and
I'm sure I'm not one to listen to gossip. Some say
he's fallen into disgrace, others that he's been
jilted by one of those fine town madams. But I
don't like the way he behaves. Going about with
Mr. Pursey takes up the mornings and then he
spends quite a bit of time with Lady Mary,
teaching her to ride. So happy she is it shines out of
her, having him spend his time with her, poor little
soul, and her terrified of horses and always has
been. But it's at night, after she's in her bed, that
he just sits, brooding. Doesn't read, doesn't drink,
won't go visiting nor receive callers. Just sits
staring into space or paces the floor, so Mr.
Johnstone says, for he's caught him at it when he
went in to see if the fire needed replenishing or if
anything was required. Now that's not natural in a
young man not yet twenty-five and I don't like it.
Something's pressing on his mind. And who's to
know what may come of it? His father was the
same after he lost his wife—and look what
happened to him."

Her lugubrious expression strongly hinted that
the late Viscount Stapleford had put a period to his

existence. In actual fact he had gone off on a long sea voyage to the Indies, leaving his infant daughter and nine-year-old son in the care of their grandparents. He had been so unfortunate as to take a pestilent fever and die of it, but Mrs. Graham was a true romantic and much preferred her own version with its suggestion of a broken heart.

Nanty frowned over the re-threading of her needle. "Where is his lordship now?" she enquired.

"Out with his sister. He still has the pony on a leading rein but declares that soon she will be fit to go alone. I'm sure I hope she may have the strength for it, but she is still sadly frail and soon droops and sickens. I've never seen her so bright and gay as she has been since his lordship's coming and only hope it does not presage some dire illness. It is often so with the delicate ones. They blossom to vivid beauty before they fade for ever."

Dear Aggie, thought her friend affectionately. She was devoted to her little mistress and would gladly sacrifice both leisure and comfort to serve her, but she *did* love to dwell on the gloomy side. Lizzie was looking quite distressed. She had always had a fondness for little Lady Mary, pitying the child's sickly habit and the restricted life that she led. They had met by chance when they were but children. Lizzie, the elder by a scant two years, had been permitted to wander in the picture gallery and had come upon the younger girl staring solemnly at the Gainsborough portrait of her Mama. Each had taken a shy liking to the other, Lizzie maternally protective to the younger child despite her lofty station, Lady Mary wistfully drawn to the vivid colour and vitality of the village girl. Their lives had rarely converged but Lizzie had always maintained her interest in the frail youngster at the Place.

"Then if all the family are out, may Lizzie stroll through the gallery and the saloons?" asked Nanty, wanting to talk freely with her friend uninhibited by eagerly receptive ears.

"Indeed she may," granted Mrs. Graham cordially. "If his lordship should chance to return earlier than expected he would but take her for one of the maids." She looked approvingly at the girl's neat grey dress and spotless cap and apron. "And a very seemly appearance she presents," she said kindly. "I daresay that dragon of a Miss Parminter will be lying in wait for Lady Mary, declaring that she has neglected her Italian or her piano-forte practice and must make it up at once. A scholarly woman she may be, but far too strict in her notions to my way of thinking."

These revolutionary sentiments were quite unsuitable for young ears. Whatever Mrs. Graham's view, the governess was a fixed part of the hierarchy and must be treated with proper respect by the lower orders. Already Lizzie's grey eyes were bright with interest. Hastily Nanty dismissed the child to her wanderings, wondering for perhaps the hundredth time what mischievous freak of her heritage had endowed her with this yearning for the lofty rooms and echoing galleries and for the treasures of art and literature with

which they were furnished. Perhaps her earliest
years had been passed in such surroundings. Ever
since Nanty had first brought her to the Place, a
child too young to be left alone at home, she had
seemed to take naturally to its grandeur and was
good as gold when permitted to wander about
freely.

Today she ran light-footed down the short
staircase that connected the housekeeper's room
with the musicians' gallery, wondering eagerly if
the holland covers that had always shrouded the
furniture in the main apartments would have been
removed. She had sometimes peeped beneath the
covers and lovingly fingered the thick satins and
damasks with which chairs and sofas were
covered. It would be delightful to see them revealed
in all their glowing beauty. But a peep into the
drawing-room proved disappointing. It was very
apparent that his lordship had no intention of
entertaining in the grand manner. Both furnish-
ings and chandeliers still wore their ghost-like
wrappings. She left the place to its dreams of
ancient splendour and walked along the gallery
which circled the first floor and then swept down to
the hall in a magnificent staircase. But with one
foot already pointed to the descent she hesitated.
How shocking it would be if the door should
suddenly open to admit Lord Stapleford. He might,
as Mrs. Graham had suggested, take her for one of
the maids—but such insignificant creatures did
not use the main staircase. Then the solemn little
face under the prim cap lit to a mischievous

twinkle. She turned and ran back along the gallery
to her own special bit of Stapleford Place, to the
discovery that had enthralled her childhood.

In one of the small saloons, quite a humble one,
such as might have been used by the daughters of
the house before they were fully "out" the fireplace
was flanked by a large alcove which had once been
a secret room. There was no secret about it now
since the panelling which had concealed it in long
ago dangerous days had been removed and the
alcove itself shelved out to hold such books and
knick-knacks as its occupants cherished. The
discovery which had so enchanted the child Lizzie,
was the fact that the place contained a peephole,
which none of the grown-ups who ruled her world
seemed to know about, perhaps because they were
all too tall to realise that one could set an eye to the
heart of a certain carved flower and see right
through the wall to the outside world. No doubt
this view had kept the hidden occupant of the
secret room informed of any happenings in that
outside world that might threaten his safety. In
Lizzie's childhood—for now, at sixteen, she considered herself quite grown-up—the peephole had
been disappointingly lacking in incident. No one
ever seemed to use the library on Thursday
afternoons and such visitors as came to the Place
did not use the front drive. She had had to make do
with creatures of her own lively invention, pic-
turing fugitive cavaliers or Jacobites galloping
furiously for the safety of the secret room. Today,
for the first time it would serve a real purpose in
enabling her to scan the terrain for the presence of

the enemy. She chuckled at her own foolish imagining. It was quite a shock to discover that she now had to kneel in order to set her eyes to the peephole. No wonder the adults had never noticed it!

For a moment she did not see the tall figure outlined against the window. Then she drew in a sharp breath of apprehension. Instinct had not played her false. This could only be Viscount Stapleford. No one else could look so completely at home and though she had never seen him in her life before she was quite sure of his identity. So absorbed was she in studying his appearance— his height, his olive skin, and hair almost black, so different from his sister's indeterminate fairness, that she quite forgot how wrong it was to be spying on someone who was unaware of being watched. Indeed, as he left the window and began to pace up and down the floor in just the fashion that Mrs. Graham had so graphically described, he did not seem to the watcher to be a real person at all, but a character out of a play or a book who was acting out his part according to the description given.

Jervase, wrestling with the problem of a delicate little sister whose spirit was gallant and gay beyond her strength, guiltily conscious of long years of neglect when he had scarcely given the child a thought, paced on steadily and wondered how he could make amends. He had returned early because the pony had loosened a shoe and there was no other beast in the stable sufficiently docile and gentle for his purpose. He knew very well, by the tight set of Mary's lips, by the tension of the thin little hands on the reins, how much it cost her to make this effort to please him, and only persevered with the lessons because he felt that the gentle exercise and freedom from the supervision of her strict governess must be beneficial.

He sighed sharply and abandoned the problem of how to contrive a little innocent gaiety for the child, seating himself at the big writing-table and beginning to hunt for some papers that Pursey had asked him to look through. The Stapleford estate was not large, by Wrelf standards, and had never necessitated a proper estate office such as there was at Wrelf. The drawers in the big table were quite adequate to the housing of leases, estimates, receipts and correspondence connected with the running of the place. He pulled open one drawer after another but could not find the papers that Pursey had mentioned. The old steward was growing very forgetful, he thought regretfully. The last drawer of all was locked but its key was in a tray on top of the desk. The drawer had evidently been used only for the money needed for the payment of wages and expenses. It still held several rolls of coins of different denominations and at the back was a very antiquated pistol. Evidently some bygone Stapleford had taken measures to protect his cash!

Mildly amused, Jervase pulled out the fearsome piece and examined it with interest. It was not loaded. He wondered how long it had lain there and who had last fired it, balancing it in his hand and smiling at its clumsy mechanism, long outdated. He could not know that to the hidden watcher, already imbued with Mrs. Graham's gloomy prognostications, his deliberate actions spelled only one intent, and that when he laid aside the pistol and drew towards him a sheet of writing paper, every fear was confirmed. So that when the library door crashed open and a slim flying figure shot into the room and caught at his arm with urgent hands, he was considerably startled.

"My lord, my lord! Please, oh! please, don't do it!" the odd creature ejaculated.

His lordship could only surmise that one of the maids had run suddenly mad and eyed the wench in some anxiety. But she showed no sign of becoming violent, the only evidence of her distraught state being the white agonised face and a pair of huge eyes that looked almost black, so widely were their pupils distended. Presently it was borne in upon him that she was a stranger. He had a pretty good memory for faces and the staff was not so large that he would not have recalled this particular countenance if he had ever seen it before. It was a distinctive face, with its fine straight nose, wide-lipped mouth and white skin, faintly powdered with freckles.

"And who the deuce are you, and what is it that I'm not to do?" he enquired, with a calm remarkable in one presumably interrupted in the act of self-destruction.

The girl did not even notice his unusual self-possession. Her mind was wholly obsessed by her fears. "Please, my lord, don't shoot yourself," she pleaded earnestly. And added with comic solemnity, "Think how dreadfully it would distress your sister!"

Viscount Stapleford stared at her in blank amazement. Then his eye chanced to fall on the pistol that he had just laid aside and for the first time in a month he rocked with laughter. "Shoot myself? With *that* thing? Why, it isn't even loaded. And if it were, it would probably misfire or throw so wide that I would be the safest person in the room. Believe me, my good girl, I am much nicer in my requirements than to attempt destruction, my own or anyone else's with that baby blunderbuss. But you have not answered my question. Who are you? And why should you imagine me bent on suicide?"

This was dreadful. She had made a complete fool of herself and perhaps brought trouble on her friends. The vibrant urgency that had impelled her to such improper behaviour was gone and she drooped visibly, her eyes filling with shamed tears.

"Come, now," said the deep, amused voice kindly, "there is no cause to look so distressed. I promise you that I will not be angry, nor even tell anyone of your very natural mistake. But you must tell me who you are and how you came to see my actions. For I am very sure that the door was closed," and now his interest was fairly aroused.

Still she looked at him in shy distress. The question sounded so simple, so natural. But how did you tell anyone your name when you hadn't got one? "I live in the village, with Mrs. Wayburn," she faltered at last when the waiting had become unbearable. And then, in miserable humility, "I don't know my real name."

In his own bitter disillusion, Jervase was sensitive to the hurt of others. He accepted the statement without comment and pressed the point which did, indeed, seem to him of greater interest. "And how did you see what I was doing?"

Now she looked up at him naturally, animation bringing out the charm of the quaint little face, even though she coloured guiltily as she explained about the peephole and her discovery of it.

"So you have been coming about the Place since you were a child," he said thoughtfully. "And now I recall that you mentioned my sister. Are you a friend of hers?"

She must be dreaming, surely? Gentlemen— noblemen—did not ask such foolish questions. But the intent dark gaze clearly expected an answer. Humbly she explained how she had first come to meet the Lady Mary.

He was silent so long that she began to wonder if she ought to withdraw quietly without attracting any further attention from him. Then he said abruptly, "What do you do?"

She looked at him blankly. Impatiently he repeated, "You look like a maid servant or abigail of some kind. Is that your occupation?"

"I was sewing maid for Mrs. Williams at Bank Sykes," she said meekly, "but I was dismissed yesterday."

"Why?" he shot at her.

Her courage was coming back. He could not eat

her after all, and he seemed a kindly young man who would not take a mean revenge on Nanty for *her* folly and presumption. She told him, with growing freedom and enjoyment, exactly how she had come to lose her place, convulsing him once more with laughter by her description of Bertha's brown-streaked countenance. Whereupon she assured him soberly that it was no laughing matter since it would probably take the poor girl a year at least to restore her hair to its former blonde beauty.

The oddly assorted couple seemed to have reached a very comfortable degree of understanding. But the girl was shocked out of all Nanty's carefully inculcated notions of proper behaviour when Viscount Stapleford said coolly, "Would you consider a post here, as maid to my sister?"

"You can't, my lord," she said bluntly. "You can't be serious. I'm not respectable. Didn't you understand? I'm—I'm a love child. That's the polite name for it. I'm not a fit person for a lady even to talk to, let alone take into her service."

It had to be made plain, even though her heart was sick at having to reject such a prospect of paradise. Maid to the Lady Mary! It would mean living here, at the Place, in the atmosphere of beauty and dignity of which she was intuitively aware. But it was too good to be true. She was not suited to such a post, however much her heart longed for it.

"I understood you perfectly well," he said. "But I cannot see how the circumstances of your birth, over which *you* had no control, make you unfit to come into contact with my sister. On the contrary,

I perceive in you a pleasing honesty and an engaging youthfulness that predispose me strongly in your favour. My sister is too much with her elders. It is my object to provide for her some younger, gayer society. And I would point out to you that many of our noblest families are proud to boast of ancestors no more legitimate than *you* claim to be."

That was his natural kindliness speaking. He had not missed the note of hurt in the young voice when she proclaimed her nameless state. Nor did he think a simple country girl, who probably could barely read, would understand the reference. She would just accept the offered comfort without question. *This* child came back at him immediately. "Yes. I know. But in those cases the father was the king or at least a royal duke. And they are different."

He could not quite restrain a smile at this simplification of the moral code, but he passed long brown fingers over his mouth to conceal the traces of amusement. Not for worlds would he have this tender sprig of innocence see that he was laughing at her. "You seem to be remarkably worldly wise, for so young a creature," he said politely. "How old are you, by the way? And who has so carefully instructed you in the—er— difference of royalty?"

"I am turned sixteen—I think— And it was Mrs. Hetherston."

The very brevity of the replies prompted him to further questioning. Nanty had been told that she was just turned three when she first came to

Stapleford. Mrs. Hetherston he knew. She was the
Vicar's wife, and it was she, Nanty being too
tender hearted to do it herself, who had explained
her equivocal position to the child, stressing the
need for her to work hard at her lessons and equip
herself as well as possible for her solitary battle
with life. An indignant outburst some months
later when the industrious pupil had made the
accidental discovery that not all illegitimate
children were poor and homeless, that some had
even been ennobled, had produced the repressive
reply that these matters were regarded differently
when royalty was concerned—and a private
admonition to the Vicar about allowing the child
free access to a library where the less creditable
pages of history were to be found.

The Viscount studied this chance-met waif with
increasing interest and enquired into the progress
of her education under the kindly aegis of Mr.
Hetherston. It proved to be startlingly solid.
Naturally no time had been wasted on lady-like
accomplishments, but the Vicar, finding his pupil
intelligent and eager, had added a grounding in
Latin and some knowledge of French to the more
basic requirements of a sound English education.
The child was probably better read than most of
her well-born contemporaries. A new and better
scheme was formulating in his mind. He fell silent,
working it out in detail. The girl stood hesitating,
wondering whether to go or stay. He had not
dismissed her, but nothing more had been said
about employing her to wait on Lady Mary. He had
evidently accepted her profession of unsuitability.

Unconsciously she sighed a little. The little sound roused Lord Stapleford from his thoughts and he got up, smiling at her kindly and studying her appearance with frank interest. Not pretty—and perhaps that was as well in her circumstances— but her eyes were remarkably fine and there was that indefinable look of race in the clean-cut features, while the slender hands and beautifully moulded arms proclaimed aloud that here was no peasant blood.

"I have another proposition to put to you," he said pleasantly. "I realise now that my first suggestion was hardly suitable, nor would it fully serve my purpose. This second notion is much better and I hope that you will consider it carefully. You must discuss it with your foster mother and with Mr. and Mrs. Hetherston before giving me your answer. It is that you should share Mary's lessons—be in some sort her companion. No! Do not answer hastily. It is an important decision, and in fairness I must point out some of the difficulties that you would encounter. Mary's governess, for instance, may not take kindly to your inclusion in the schoolroom world. I do not think she would treat you with the cruelty and spite that you seem to have encountered at your last post, but you may find her strict, even severe. You may have difficulty with some of the maids, if they share Miss Williams's jealousy of your superior attainments. You would have to leave Mrs. Wayburn's care and come here to live. And I must tell you frankly at the outset that your speech is not quite that of a cultured person. No need to blush, child," as she hung her head. "It is only natural that you should have picked up the local brogue. But it will not do for Mary to be copying you. It is a matter that can easily be mended. But none of this will be easy for you. On the other hand you will be receiving both education and training in the ways of the polite world, and when the time comes that you wish to make a change I will do my best to help you to a suitable situation."

Not quite sure whether she was awake or dreaming and desperately self-conscious for the first time in her life, she stammered out some kind of inarticulate thanks.

"And you still have not told me your name," he reminded.

There was a moment's silence. Then she looked up at him solemnly, forgetting the new paralysing shyness in speaking of a matter that lay close to her heart. "When first I came to Nanty, she tells me, I said that my name was Lissa. She took that to be a shortened form of Elizabeth. I have always been called Lizzie, and I hate it. Do you think I could be Lissa again—if I come here to live, I mean," and her eyes glowed at the exciting prospect and all the difficulties were forgotten.

"I certainly share your preference for Lissa," he agreed. "What about your second name. Since we are having a christening, shall we change that, too?"

He had thought merely to set her at ease by a little friendly teasing and was unprepared for the reaction that his idle remark provoked. Her head went up proudly. "Indeed, no, my lord. Since

Nanty was so good as to give me her own name, which was more than my parents did for me, I will keep it and strive to bring credit on it. How could I hurt her by seeming to despise it the moment my circumstances seem like to change for the better?"

So the prim looking shy little thing had spirit enough when she was roused. And admirable instincts, too. Momentarily he was becoming more and more enamoured of his scheme. This girl would do Mary all the good in the world. He was almost prepared to back her against the formidable Miss Parminter, though he would be watchful to see that the youngster was not really oppressed. He would teach her to ride along with Mary, and there would have to be dancing lessons, too. Planning the polishing of this untried jewel that had fallen into his hands would add a piquancy to the quiet country days. He sent her off to find her foster mother, bidding her think carefully over all that he had said, but adding sincerely that he hoped her decision would be favourable. She dropped him a demure curtsey and walked sedately from the room, after which she gathered up her sober skirts and half ran, half danced upstairs to Mrs. Graham's parlour where she burst in upon the astounded occupants and poured out her tale in such a bubble of excitement that the good ladies had much ado in making head or tail of it.

Chapter 3

ALMOST A month passed before Lissa Wayburn
entered upon her new life at Stapleford Place. But
the days were so charged with blissful preparation
that they passed swiftly, even to her eager
impatience. It was not without much thought and
a number of misgivings, some openly expressed,
others denied utterance, that her friends and well
wishers were finally persuaded to permit her
acceptance of her fantastic good fortune. They
could foresee all the difficulties that the Viscount
had mentioned and a good many more, not the
least of these being the fear that the child would be
given ideas above her station. The generous whim
of a wealthy young man was not to be relied upon.
They acquitted him of any evil intent towards his
protegée, but he might easily weary of the whole
business, perhaps return to Town and his former
gay life and forget about the waif whose hopes and
ambitions he had fostered by his brief inexplicable
notice. Lord Stapleford had to spend a full hour
closeted with the Vicar in his study before that

good man was fully convinced that the scheme really *was* designed to be beneficial to both Lissa and Lady Mary. To his credit he placed them in that order. Lady Mary had a number of people to guard her welfare. He himself felt deeply responsible for Lizzie—and he must remember to call her Lissa.

Having once made up his mind, Mr. Hetherston devoted his energies to correcting the child's rustic accent, a process which she found painfully embarrassing. Her speech was so eager and fluent that it was sheer misery to be checked again and again to correct her pronunciation. The task was made all the more difficult by the fact that she was so very nearly correct. Nanty had always been particular about her speech, never permitting her to lapse into dialect, so that only the ear of a purist could detect the slightly broadened vowels, the slurred consonants and the lazy elisions. But the day did eventually dawn when suddenly she could hear the difference between her pronunciation and the Vicar's and from then on her progress was noticeable if erratic. There were times when Mr. Hetherston was hard put to it not to laugh at his earnest pupil's comical mistakes, but he was sincerely fond of her and managed to dissemble his amusement.

To make up for all this humiliation there were the clothes. The Viscount had decreed the provision of a wardrobe suitable to a young lady of good standing who was not yet 'out', and had given Mesdames Hetherston and Wayburn carte blanche in its choosing. He had some doubts about

this, fearing that they would incline towards
sparing his purse, but he could scarcely go
shopping for the girl himself so he compromised by
saying that a riding habit and several light
dresses suitable for dancing lessons must be
selected as well as more workaday clothes and
leaving the choice to them. His fears might well
have been realised, both ladies being of an
economical nature, but fortunately there was one
factor that he had left out of his reckoning. He was
giving to two childless women the opportunity to
dress a dream daughter at his expense. There could
be no denying that the experience went to their
heads, driving out customary frugality, but since
they had both good sense and good taste they
expressed their unusual extravagance in terms of
cut and quality and the result was all that could
have been wished. They began by buying day
dresses in sober colours that would not easily soil
but they both succumbed to the charm of a green
polonaise with a green and white flowered under-
dress. That would be very suitable for going to
church and for similar formal wear, they decided,
and then indulged feminine instinct to the full in
the selection of a simple yellow crepe saque and a
dainty flowered muslin for dancing lessons. Mrs.
Hetherston shook her head over the extravagance
of buying two dresses when one would really have
sufficed for a girl who had not yet done growing,
but the Viscount had definitely said "several"
which was really rather fortunate as *she* preferred
the yellow crepe while Nanty had lost her heart to
the muslin. The owner of all this new finery was

too overcome to do more than acquiesce ecstati-
cally in the decisions of her elders, which caused
Mrs. Hetherston to pat her cheek approvingly and
praise her pretty behaviour. Neither the Viscount
nor his enthusiastic assistants expected the new
clothes to make any great change in the child's
appearance. They were simply the proper wear for
the part she was called upon to play.

But in spite of the confidence born of knowing
that at least she would be suitably dressed, Lissa
felt her spirits sink on the last night that she spent
in her childhood home. All the new clothes were
packed save for a snuff brown day dress and a tiny
hat trimmed with a modest brown ribbon which
was worn tilted over the right eyebrow. The
carriage was to take her up at ten o'clock next
morning and her new life would begin. She felt sick
and shivery at the thought, and Nanty, seeing the
restless movements and the sober little face
suggested that she should take a warm bath in
front of the kitchen fire and then wash her hair
and practise dressing it in the new fashion. "For,"
as she sensibly said, "you will feel strange to be
going without your cap and your hair all loose
about your shoulders, but that is the way that
Lady Mary wears hers and his lordship wishes you
to copy her appearance in this respect."

Not even Nanty was prepared for the startling
change that the new fashion made in Lissa. Over
the years the red-gold of the childish curls had
deepened to a glorious copper colour, but since the
hair had always been strained back from the thin
little wedge of a face and tightly braided under the

prim cap, no one had realised its beauty until now
it hung about the girl's shoulders in all its shining
glory. No need for crimping tongs here. You could
do anything with it—except suppress its suggestion of the deepest joys of living and loving. It was
scandalous hair, thought Nanty uneasily, such as
would put the wickedest thoughts into men's
heads, and yet the child was as good a girl as ever
stepped. Magdalene hair, she said to herself, with
some dim memory of legend. The deep waves swept
back from the white brow and formed themselves
into natural ringlets as their owner twisted them
carelessly round her fingers, while delicate tendrils sprang back from her temples in tiny rings of
new minted gold. Then Lissa looked up at her with
the old, rueful grimace and said, "Still carrots,
Nanty! Do you remember when I used to pray
every night for it to go dark, and how cross you
used to be? You said I should be content with what
the good Lord had given me." And then she
giggled. "But at least I won't use walnut juice! I
can promise you that." And Nanty's sudden fears
were calmed, for the child was still her own loving,
innocent child.

Nevertheless, even if she had done it deliberately, she could not have chosen better than the
dark stuffs of the new dresses to set off that
wonderful hair. It was with a sense of startled
disbelief that Lord Stapleford received his new-
fashioned protegée. In plain, beautifully cut brown
dress and the tiny hat which had suddenly become
saucy when perched on the coppery curls, she was
quite a different creature from the thin plain little

piece of their first meeting. Then he realised that
she was almost paralysed with shyness. He
complimented her with grave courtesy on her
becoming appearance and assured her two anxious sponsors that they had perfectly understood
his wishes and had carried them out to a nicety.

There was a brief farewell to Mrs. Hetherston, a
loving hug for Nanty and a reminder that it was
not long till Thursday, when they would meet
again, and then she was left to fight her dragons
alone.

At least Lady Mary could not be described as a
dragon though there was an unexpected shyness
between them, Lady Mary being startled at the
change in Lissa's appearance and Lissa tongue-
tied because she had forgotten to ask Nanty how
she should address the younger girl. Would it be
more courteous to use the formal "your ladyship"
of their previous acquaintance or was she supposed to use the more familiar "Lady Mary"? The
Viscount had arranged that his sister should be
delivered from the tyranny of lessons for this first
morning and, sensing the awkwardness between
the two, now suggested that Mary should show her
new companion the room that had been allotted
her and help her to unpack and settle in, feeling
that the two would manage much better without
his society. Lady Mary put out an impulsive hand
to catch Lissa's and her sallow little face lit up as
she said, "Oh, yes! Do come and see. I hope you will
like it. I asked Mrs. Graham to put you in the room
next to mine. It's not very big because Miss
Parminter has the big one at the other side, but it's

a corner room and has a turret window." She pulled at Lissa's hand impatiently, scarcely allowing her time to drop a polite curtsey to Lord Stapleford who smiled at his animated little sister and felt rather more hopeful for the success of his scheme.

Had he been privileged to hear the exchanges between the two once the bedroom door was safely closed behind them, his confidence would have been complete. Within five minutes they were both chattering away like magpies, Lissa exclaiming in delight over the turret room which made her feel, she said, like a princess in a medieval romance, and Mary instantly exclaiming that she looked exactly like one, a remark which could hardly fail to please. The business of unpacking took an unconscionably long time, there were so many things to be explained and discussed, so many delightful plans to be made. Lissa even summoned courage to lay the problem of correct address before the person most concerned. Mary looked wistful. "I wish you could call me Mary," she said slowly. "Then I could almost believe you were my sister. But I don't think Miss Parminter would allow it. She is a great stickler for proper form. It will have to be Lady Mary when she is there, but we can do as we like when we are alone."

In answer to Lissa's anxious questions she said that Miss Parminter was strict but fair. One had to work hard but she could make the lessons interesting. The schoolroom maid, Janet, was Mrs. Graham's niece and was a dear. "Though I don't like Kate, who waits on us when Janet has her day off. She's sulky. But that won't be for ages yet," she ended cheerfully and suggested that they had better go to the schoolroom to find Miss Parminter or she would be sending to enquire why they were so long.

The governess greeted Lissa with cool civility and, like everyone else, glanced thoughtfully at the riot of copper curls, so that Lissa put up a nervous hand to smooth them back. She asked one or two questions as to the point the girl had reached in her studies and seemed reasonably satisfied with the answers, then went on to strike dismay into her heart by saying, "In the matter of your speech I must ask you to be particularly careful until time and assiduous practice have polished away its rusticity. Lord Stapleford has announced his intention of attending to this matter himself, since he esteems it of great importance. You are to spend half an hour each evening in reading aloud to him and in recounting the events of your day. I need hardly point out to you that you are a very privileged young person and must show your gratitude by diligent application to your studies."

Lissa stammered out something disjointed but breathless with gratitude, and shook in her shoes. It had been bad enough when the Vicar had pounced on every tiny fault, but the prospect that now faced her was appalling. Heartily she wished herself back in her comfortable obscurity.

"Tonight, however," went on Miss Parminter, "his lordship has arranged that you shall both dine with him and dinner has been set forward especially so that you may do so. No doubt he wishes to satisfy himself that your manners are not such as to disgust the polite world. On that head," she added in a more kindly tone, "I believe you need not be anxious. Some small points may stand in need of correction, but I am assured that you have been very well brought up by your foster mother. You may go now. A nuncheon will be served to you in the schoolroom in half an hour's time and your riding lesson will be at three o'clock. Be sure that you do not keep his lordship waiting."

Getting into a riding habit was still a complicated business for Lissa despite some previous practice, but with Mary's help and a good deal of giggling the pair of them were ready in good time. And the lesson itself was sheer joy to the tyro, even though she was only permitted to make friends with the pony and then to sit on his back while her tutor walked him gently round the stable yard. The Viscount was delighted to see how his sister—with more than a month's equestrian tuition to her credit—seemed to shed all her own nervousness when trying to help Lissa, pushing away the pony's inquisitive nose when he snuffed at her breast almost absently instead of flinching away as she would have done only yesterday. As for Lissa, quite fearless where animals were concerned, she only wished the lesson might go on longer, though his lordship warned her, with some amusement, that even as it was she would probably feel stiff and sore tomorrow. With childish memories of stolen rides on the farm horses, Lissa knew all about *that* but felt it was well worth it, especially when she received a brief commendation, the Viscount being good enough to say that in spite of her advanced age she might yet make a horsewoman, since at least she didn't use the reins as a balancing pole or saw at the pony's mouth.

A sympathetic Mrs. Graham had seen to it that the early dinner which had been ordered was as simple as possible. Indeed the chef had been positively shocked by its miserly nature and she had been put to some pains to coax him back to good humour.

"A first course of no more than five dishes with only three in the second course, and no more than four side dishes? His lordship will think we are trying to starve him!"

Mrs. Graham had spoken soothingly of the Lady Mary's delicacy, saying that they must not have the poor child's digestion upset by too many rich dishes, while as for his lordship, he never seemed to care what he ate, for not once since his arrival had he seen fit to compliment the artist who created all these palate-tickling delights for his delectation. However, if Jacques felt so strongly about it, he might add a whim-wham to the second course. The young ladies, at least, would appreciate that.

So dinner was not such an ordeal after all, especially as his lordship told the servants that they might withdraw after bringing in the second course and allowed the girls to serve themselves with such items as they fancied while he finished his wine in leisurely contemplation. There was a slight set-back when he idly suggested that they had better both take lessons in carving, but the two horror stricken faces that lifted to his so touched his sympathies that he hastily added that there would be plenty of time for that later. Much relieved, the young ladies returned to the discussion of the whim-wham, which had met with their entire approval. The rest of the meal passed in amicable discussion of the art of riding and an argument as to how soon Lissa might hope to dispense with the ignominy of the leading rein.

Nevertheless, after the tea tray had been brought in, and both girls in turn had tried their prentice hands at dispensing that stimulating fluid, Lissa, at any rate, was thankful to obey the dismissal to bed which followed. In all her short life she had never been so tired. Even pig killing at the Williams's, when everyone had been pressed into service to reduce the great carcasses to the several forms of pork products, had not been so exhausting as this, she decided, with a shudder of revulsion for the memory. Yet she had done nothing that was recognisable as work. All she had done was try to avoid falling into the social pitfalls that she sensed all about her. His lordship had been right when he said it would not be easy. It was very difficult indeed. But it was exciting, challenging, and with every scrap of her being she was determined on success. She tucked the neat braids of hair into the dainty cap that Nanty had so lovingly embroidered, climbed into bed and blew out the candle.

Chapter 4

It was a month before Miss Parminter capitulated. When she did, her surrender was whole-hearted, though the only outward change was a slightly increased gruffness in such remarks as she addressed to Lissa.

Edith Parminter had never been loved or wanted. Born to parents who had eagerly desired a son, she had been handed over to a succession of nursemaids who supplied her material needs and, so long as she gave them no trouble, largely ignored her. She was a plain little girl, silent and withdrawn, with a secret adoration for her handsome, heedless father who was carelessly kind to her if he chanced to notice her presence. By the time that she was ten she had lost both her parents and had passed into the charge of a great-uncle who, on finding that his nephew had died deep in debt, accepted the legacy with grudging resentment, and, on the assumption that such a sour little piece was unlikely to marry with no dowry to sweeten the dose, had seen that she was given a

good education, found her a respectable post as a
governess and washed his hands of all further
responsibility. It said much for Miss Parminter's
sense of fairness that she did not blame anyone for
the bleakness of her life and was, indeed, grateful
to her Great-uncle Carnforth for putting himself to
so much expense on her behalf. She was genuinely
fond of the Lady Mary and extremely conscien-
tious in the discharge of her duties, but it never
occurred to her that the child would have re-
sponded ardently to a more open affection.

She had viewed the irruption of Lissa Wayburn
into their well regulated days with considerable
doubt and had watched, hawk-eyed, for any sign of
presumption in the girl. She found her shy, but not
timid, eager to learn and to do all that was asked of
her. Her understanding was good though she was
not in any way bookish unless one counted a
marked taste for history, a preference which
developed into positive fervour when the theme
touched on Stapleford Place. It seemed to be an
obsession with her, thought the governess curi-
ously. She was already far better acquainted with
its fabled past than was the Lady Mary, and on
one occasion, when taken to task for day-dreaming
when she should have been practising her pen-
manship, had apologised frankly and then explained, with that disarmingly candid smile of
hers, "I was thinking how wonderful it is that I am
actually living here in this lovely place. Sometimes
I still cannot believe that I am not dreaming."

Miss Parminter had been touched by the
simplicity, the utter lack of pretension in the girl's

attitude. She had already accorded her respect to
the determination with which Lissa struggled to
overcome her difficulty in speaking correctly. Her
embarrassment was plain to see, yet she never
resented the frequent request for repetition, accepting correction quietly and then practising until she
had it right. She was fortunate in having a quick
ear, thought Miss Parminter; less fortunate in her
sensitive spirit. A coarser fibre would have
laughed over the mistakes she made. Lissa
flushed, set her lips, and tried again. She bore no
malice, accepting the humiliation as the price she
paid for her many advantages.

At this stage Miss Parminter allowed her
natural sympathy for a girl even less wanted than
herself to soften her strict impartiality. She, at
least, had a name to which she knew herself
entitled, and even a blood relation—such as he
was. Lissa had nothing save what she could win
for herself. Keeping a firm restraint on undue
sentimentality, Miss Parminter continued to
watch her two charges far more closely than they
guessed. She saw that Lissa was genuinely fond of
Lady Mary, tender to her physical weakness,
encouraging her in all her interests, delighted
when these were mildly mischievous and perfectly
ready to accept all the blame. That was wrong, of
course, but funnily enough it had the right results,
for Lady Mary refused to shelter under Lissa's
protection, stoutly asserting her own responsibility for her own misdeeds.

There came a day when the morning's lessons
had chanced to include the tale of how the then

Lord of Stapleford—long before the acquisition of the Marquisate of Wrelf—had held by the House of York, dying on Bosworth Field in a vain attempt to bring succour to his rightful sovereign. Lissa had been enthralled, her great eyes almost black in her absorption, and, at the end of the lesson, unusually silent. Having waited in vain for the usual eager question or comment, Miss Parminter dismissed her pupils to tidy themselves for luncheon. A minute later Lissa had come back, walking slowly, still half a-dream, and had put out both hands towards her, saying, "Thank you. It was wonderful. You made him live again." And then, as though there was no more to be said, had turned abruptly on her heel and walked out of the room.

Miss Parminter had been quite taken aback, but no one could help being flattered by so sincere a tribute. She had immediately acquitted the girl of any deliberate attempt to please. The outburst had been too natural, too abrupt. Nor had she waited to see the result of her words. She had felt impelled to say them—had done so. But it was at this point that Miss Parminter abandoned her impartial attitude and decided that Lissa Wayburn was an honest and lovable creature and that the Viscount had indeed chosen well when selecting her to companion his sister.

This favourable opinion was confirmed by an incident which occurred two or three days later. The schoolroom at Stapleford Place had modern sash windows instead of the small-paned casements that had so delighted Lissa in her turret room, and Miss Parminter, who had a most

unfashionable fancy for fresh air, always insisted
on these being opened as soon as lessons were done
so that the room might be thoroughly "sweetened,"
as she termed it. Lissa, coming into the room in
search of a book to read because heavy rain had
caused the riding lesson to be abandoned, found
the windows still open and the rain driving in over
a table piled with books and soaking the curtains
and floor covering. She ran across to the window to
close it only to find that the sash had jammed and
she could not move it. It had not previously
happened that she had needed to summon any of
the servants to her assistance but in this case there
was no option and she pulled the bell without a
second thought and then hurried back to the table
to rescue the books before they were quite ruined.
She heard the door open but did not look round
until an aggressive voice said, "It's you, is it, Miss
Smarty-boots? Ringing for the servants as though
you were a lady born and making me run up all
those stairs. Think yourself wonderful, don't you,
cocked up over us all and living as high as a coach
horse, and you not so much as born in wedlock.
Why, my mother wouldn't have you in our house,
as well you do know. And I suppose if I speak the
truth about your fine job here you'll run to old
Graybag telling tales and get me turned off.
Well—what do you want, seeing as how I'm here?"

Miss Parminter, who had suddenly remembered
the open window and hurried from her room to
close it, heard this vulgar diatribe with shocked
disgust and deliberately waited to see how Lissa
would deal with it.

She heard the girl say, with quiet dignity, "I am sorry to have put you to any trouble, Kate, but I could not close the window and as you may see for yourself the rain is spoiling everything. Perhaps we could manage to shut it between us."

A contemptuous snort was the only answer that Kate vouchsafed to that. Miss Parminter heard the window crash down with a force that must have come near to shattering the glass. "There, Lady Lily Fingers! Too genteel even to shut a window. You, that's the laughing stock of the village, with your high and mighty airs, as though everyone didn't know all about you! My mother says you'll go the way of the light-skirt that bore you—and you may be starting high with one of the nobs but it's in the gutters you'll end when his lordship tires of you."

Even Miss Parminter was stunned by the virulence of the servant's attack. And to dare to speak so of his lordship! She drew herself up to her full imposing height and was about to march into the room to annihilate the insolent wretch when she realised that her help was not needed. Lissa's voice was perfectly steady and gentle but there was an icy determination in it that carried complete conviction, even to the recalcitrant Kate.

"You may say what you please about *me*, Kate, if it gives you any pleasure. It does not hurt *me*. And even in our school days you will recall that I was no tale bearer. But if you ever dare to repeat your foul insinuations against Lord Stapleford, or if I have cause to believe that you are spreading your disgusting tales to smear the name of an honourable man, it is not to Mrs. Graham that I shall carry my story but to his lordship himself. I give you this one plain warning. You may go. But remember what I have said for I mean every word of it."

"There will be no need for you to go to such lengths, my child," said Miss Parminter, sailing into the room to confound a deflated Kate. "I heard every word that passed between you, and I do not subscribe to your delicate scruples about tale bearing—at least not in such a case as this. I think that you may safely start packing your box, Kate, for I am sure that when Mrs. Graham hears of your outrageous insolence she will not have you in the house a moment longer. Nor need you hope for a reference."

Kate tried to brazen it out, tossing her head impudently and swaggering out of the room with her nose in the air. Inwardly she was already quaking at the thought of what her mother would say when she heard that her daughter had been dismissed without a character. Mrs. Stucker had been delighted when Kate had been taken into service at the Place, the first of their family to achieve that distinction. Such posts were generally limited to the small coterie of families that had served the Wyncasters in one capacity or another for the past two hundred years. Only the fact that the ladies Bell, Wood and Truby had produced eight sons between them and never a daughter had given Kate her chance. And now she had made a fatal error and lost it. Her mother would never get over it, after the way she had boasted around the

village. And it was all the fault of that horried
stuck-up Lissa Wayburn, whom she had always
detested. Well—she would not forget. She would
find some way of getting her own back on the girl
who had caused her downfall, thought Kate, now
working herself into a righteous indignation and
mentally rehearsing the version of the tale that
she would present to her mother.

In this design she was frustrated by the
forethought of Mrs. Graham who had been
dissatisfied from the outset with the girl's attitude
to her work and her employers and was further
incensed by Miss Parminter's report of the conversation that she had overheard. "Old Graybag,
indeed," she said grimly. "Leave it to me, Miss. I'll
see that the impudent baggage gets her come-
uppance. I'll take her home myself, this very
afternoon, and I'll see that Bab Stucker hears the
truth of the matter."

The Viscount did not concern himself greatly
over the domestic organisation of the Place,
assuming that Mrs. Graham would continue to
exercise that benign autocracy which ensured his
comfort and drew a discreet veil over the means by
which it was achieved. He was therefore much
intrigued when the unobtrusive ruling deity of his
establishment suddenly requested an interview
with him and even more so when she asked that
Miss Parminter should be present. He heard their
story with a mixture of mild disgust and some
satisfaction and willingly endorsed the action
taken by both ladies. Since they had agreed
together beforehand that all reference to Kate's

shocking insinuations about his lordship should
be tactfully omitted from their account, her offence
figured as "insulting remarks about Miss
Wayburn's birth, parentage and morals". This
sort of thing he had foreseen and was pleased to
learn that his protegée had met it with more tact
and dignity than might reasonably have been
expected. But on voicing this opinion to Miss
Parminter after Mrs. Graham had withdrawn he
was rather taken aback by that lady's firm shake
of the head and the indulgent smile that she might
have bestowed on a rather backward pupil.

"She behaved *exactly* as I would have expected,
my lord. Whatever the truth of her birth no one
who knows her would dispute the fact that she is
unquestionably a lady in the best sense of the
word."

Lord Stapleford was quite overset by this
unexpected encomium. He wondered how the
miracle had been achieved. To have the strict,
difficult Miss Parminter, the stickler for correct
form, taking up the cudgels on behalf of a village
brat of questionable ancestry was something he
had never hoped to hear. It inspired him with a
sudden interest in Lissa's history. No doubt she
had told him all that she knew but very probably
her foster mother was better informed. It would be
interesting to try what he could find out about this
rara avis.

But Nanty, tactfully approached, denied all
knowledge, and he was brought to believe that she
spoke truth. She had answered an advertisement
in the columns of a newspaper, asking for a

respectable motherly woman to take charge of a child. Agnes Graham had brought it to her notice, just at the time she was mourning her husband who had been killed in action between the *Serapis* and the *Bonhomme Richard*. It had seemed to her like an answer to prayer, providing her with a reason for living and the means to go on living in her own small home. Her application had been successful. The lawyer, a Mr. Whitehead, had travelled into Wiltshire to assure himself that the accommodation and the care that she could offer were adequate and had pronounced himself satisfied. She told, in voluble detail, of Lissa's arrival and of the infrequent but magnificent presents; of the regular payments and the sudden cessation of all communication. Finding him a sympathetic listener, she even confided her own speculations as to the child's history. He nodded thoughtfully and thanked her for her frankness, but went away disappointed and more than ever curious.

To add to his frustration he now perceived a new reserve in Lissa's attitude during their evening lessons. Once her first agonising selfconsciousness had been conquered she had actually begun to enjoy these, defending herself vigorously when she had mis-pronounced some word and roundly declaring that English was the most ridiculous language, not near so sensible and logical as French, creating rules only in order to make exceptions to them. When his lordship solemnly suggested that in the present state of war between the two countries such an opinion was tantamount to treason, she chuckled—a delightful little gurgle of merriment that he enjoyed provoking. Since he himself was responsible for it, he found her naïve enjoyment of her new life subtly flattering and also highly educational. His own liberal beliefs had been the lofty ideals of youth. He had proclaimed the equal rights of all mankind, but he'd never dreamed of a world in which warm water was a luxury to be attained only by considerable toil and then to be savoured appreciatively, while books to read and a candle to read them by were such self-indulgence as to verge on the sinful. And this was a girl who had been well cared for—who had never gone hungry or cold. He found himself enjoying his own comfortable existence with greater zest, seeing each small luxury through Lissa's eyes and valuing it accordingly.

So he was deeply disappointed when her engaging confidences, her spirited arguments and the laughter that lurked in the grey eyes even if it did not always find utterance, were suddenly exchanged for the polite reserve with which she now treated him. He was not to know how roughly Kate's coarse suggestions had opened her innocent eyes to the ambiguity of her situation. Charm he never so wisely there was no restoration of the former easy relationship and he was eventually driven to enquire if he had offended her in some way.

She did not pretend to misunderstand him, but her eyes were lowered to the hands lying lightly clasped in her lap as she said slowly, "Indeed, no, my lord. But now that I am accustomed to the ways of polite society I realise that my manners were much too free. Because, in your courtesy, you have treated me as you treat your sister, I have used towards you a familiarity bordering on the presumptuous. This is a grave fault and a sad return for your generosity. I beg your pardon for it and am trying to govern my conduct more seemly."

"If you're going to talk that kind of fustian, my girl," said his lordship wrathfully, "you will make me regret that I ever invited you to come to the Place. I never thought to hear such arrant nonsense from one I judged to be a sensible wench. You are doing an excellent job with Mary. She is happier than ever she was in her life. How else should I treat you but as her equal? As for my "generosity," it is fortunate for you, Miss Wayburn, that I am *not* your brother. Many an impudent small sister had had her ears boxed on lesser provocation. Let us have no more of this rodomontade."

She smiled and asked him what that meant. There was a glow of content in the fine eyes when he praised her influence on Mary, but it was evident that she did not accept his reassurances; that the old confiding trust was gone. He realised that she was troubled in some way but it seemed to him wiser not to press her too closely. He settled himself to the evening's task, trusting to time and patience to set all to rights.

Chapter 5

THE CHANGE in Lissa was in part explained when Mr. Hetherston came to call upon his lordship. That good man had pondered long before committing himself to an interview which was bound to be difficult, demanding of much diplomacy, a quality which he felt was not his strong suit. But the unpleasant hints and rumours which had reached his ears indicated that it was clearly his duty to intervene and neither the awkwardness of the business nor the likelihood that he would hopelessly alienate his patron's grandson must be allowed to deflect him from the course indicated by his conscience.

The preliminary courtesies of a morning call having been dealt with, he set about his task without delay. In frank terms he related the stories that were going about the village, consequent, he suspected, upon the dismissal of Kate Stucker. But these, he informed his host, were comparatively unimportant. The Williams family had joyfully joined in the defamatory chorus but neither they nor the Stuckers carried much weight with local opinion, the Stuckers, in fact, being heartily disliked. The malicious gossip would die a natural death when Kate Stucker found fresh employment and Bertha Williams's hair resumed its natural colour. There was an uncanonical twinkle in the good man's eyes as he confided to his lordship that only the strongest representations on the part of his wife had prevented him from preaching a sermon on the dangers of vanity. His lordship grinned companionably but was too much disturbed by his report to enter fully into the humour of the situation. Nor did he find much comfort in soothing assurances that Mrs. Wayburn was well able to deal with open slanders and had far more friends and supporters in the village than had her enemies, for Hetherston had warned that there was worse to come. He controlled his mounting anger and waited, with ominous patience, to hear it.

The Vicar plunged on courageously. "What is much more unfortunate is that some of these rumours seem to have percolated beyond the village. I have received a number of hints from members of my congregation, and on Sunday morning Mrs. Wetherley actually took me to task for countenancing your flagrantly scandalous conduct. I assured her that there was nothing in the least scandalous but, on the contrary, a great deal that was both admirable and charitable, but I fear that I did not succeed in convincing her," he ended sadly.

His lordship got up and crossed to the long

windows that opened on to the terrace, turning his back on the Vicar. It might seem impolite, but it was better than giving vent to the pithy description of Mrs. Wetherley's ancestry, birth, morals and conduct which was seething on the tip of his tongue and was certainly not suited to clerical ears. He stood there for some minutes, lean, strong fingers tapping a brisk tattoo on the glass, what time he mastered his temper. When at last he turned and came back to the hearth, murmuring a word of apology, his voice was perfectly controlled, but there was a look in his eye and a set to his mouth that reminded the Vicar forcibly of the Most Honourable the Marquis of Wrelf in one of his black rages. Perhaps there was not the same sound and fury, but never before had Mr. Hetherston seen in him this strong resemblance to his grandsire. He was uneasily aware that he would not care to cross this easygoing friendly young man in such a mood and devoutly hoped that his tactful persuasions would suffice.

"I would have thought that the local—gentry—" said Lord Stapleford icily, his tone turning the word into an insult—"even if they credited me with the seduction of an innocent child under my own roof, might at least have considered it unlikely that I would permit my mistress to become the intimate friend of my sister. However I accept your word for it that they do so believe. As for Mrs. Wetherley, she and my grandfather are bosom bows, and her nature is such that she would delight in making mischief if she could. If she goes tattling to *him* she is more likely to receive a sharp set-down," he added thoughtfully, a gleam of cold amusement in his eyes as he recalled his last conversation with his grandfather. "But that is hardly to the point. It is Miss Wayburn's good name that we have to consider. Let me say at once that I would be loath to disturb the present arrangement. So far as my sister is concerned it is working far better than I had dared to hope. I believe that Miss Wayburn, too, is benefiting from the wider opportunities that are open to her. Miss Parminter, I know, is much impressed with her abilities and character."

That certainly gave the business a new aspect. The Vicar had entertained some notion of suggesting that Lissa might be sent to a respectable seminary as compensation for losing her agreeable position. In view of the Viscount's remarks he now dismissed this solution and offered his rather more complicated plan.

"I beg you will not take offence, my lord, if I speak freely," he began with considerable diffidence. "Both of us have Miss Wayburn's interests at heart and if I seem to rebuke you for certain ill-judged actions I trust that you will bear that fact in mind." He looked up, half appealingly, at the set countenance. The dark eyes met his with a trace of hauteur. Viscount Stapleford was not accustomed to having any of his actions called in question. The Vicar sighed. At least the young man seemed prepared to listen, and that was more than his grandfather would have done.

"In your dealings with Miss Wayburn I believe you to have acted on impulse—a generous, a chivalrous impulse, I make no doubt, but hastily conceived. There would have been no harm in that, since the girl was quite adequately chaperoned by Miss Parminter. The trouble has arisen largely because of your behaviour when first you came to Stapleford. Had you mixed with such of the local people as feel themselves entitled to be received at Stapleford Place, accepted some of their invitations and entertained in return, eaten their dinners and danced with their daughters—perhaps, especially, danced with their daughters—I believe that you would have escaped this scandal broth entirely. You must be aware that your unexpected arrival here caused a considerable stir. A good many reasons for it were imagined and freely discussed, and your behaviour in shutting yourself away added fuel to the fire of speculation. Add to this that you are one of the most eligible young men in the country. Heirs to Marquisates do not grow on every bush. I daresay every Mama of a marriageable daughter within twenty miles has bought her girl a new gown at the very least in the hope that she might catch your eye. Instead of which you shun them all and take into your household a girl of unknown birth and doubtful respectability. Yes, I know the girl is a good girl, as innocent as your own sister. But do you wonder at it that disappointment and jealousy were only too eager to seize upon the first suggestion of scandal and to spread it abroad with relish?"

He had begun his speech diffidently enough but had warmed to the task as he went on, forgetting the culprit's exalted rank and speaking as he might have done to a son of his own in similar circumstances. Now he was guiltily aware that he had quite forgotten the respectful approach that was his lordship's due and prepared himself to endure the expected set-down with decent composure.

It did not come. Glancing up at that dark forbidding countenance he saw that the look of arrogance was gone. His lordship was pulling thoughtfully at a rather long upper lip, and as he met the Vicar's doubtful glance he even smiled a little. "I do seem to have made rather a cake of myself, don't I, Sir?" he said pleasantly. "No excuse to offer either. If I had given the matter a moment's thought I should have known how it would be. Now pray don't think me a conceited coxcomb as well as a congenital idiot. I mean only that I should have remembered how it is in small communities. You are quite right, of course. I should have shown myself at the Wetherleys' musical soirée and gone about more in general, but to speak truth I came down here in search of an anodyne that might heal my self-disgust and hoped to find it in solitude and hard work. No need to look distressed," he interpolated cheerfully, "I find myself recovered almost unaware. And now that you have rung your peal over me, tell me how I may mend matters."

Mr. Hetherston blinked, scarcely believing that he had heard aright. In his younger, more poverty-pinched, days, he had frequently eked out a meagre pittance by tutoring scions of the nobility who found difficulty in gaining admission to the

academic groves. He had grown accustomed to
arrogance, even rudeness, and at best to a total
lack of consideration for his own sensibilities. The
Viscount was, of course, considerably older than
the unlicked cubs of Mr. Hetherston's memory, but
to accept in good part the raking down that he had
received and then to admit its justification argued
a sweetness of disposition both rare and admirable. Since the Vicar had never been privileged to
hear the Marquis of Wrelf in full flow of vitupera-
tion he was blissfully unaware that to Lord
Stapleford his rebuke had seemed excessively
mild.

He beamed upon this promising young man
with genuine liking. "If you could bring yourself to
do so, it is not too late to rectify the position," he
suggested tentatively. "It would, of course, be fatal
to plunge into a sudden whirl of social activity, but
attendance at one or two functions with perhaps
some show of hospitality in return would do much
to redeem your reputation. If, without labouring
the point, you could casually mention the improvement in your sister's health and spirits now that
she has a companion of her own age to share in
her activities, and even drop a hint that it is this
comfortable state of affairs that now leaves you
free to pursue your own inclinations, I feel that you
would soon be restored to favour with Mrs.
Wetherley and that Miss Wayburn would come to
be regarded as a positive benefactress."

The Viscount regarded him with considerable
respect. "You know, Sir," he said with a grin, "I
cannot help feeling that you have mistaken your

path in life. You have either chosen the wrong
profession or the wrong Church. In the Diplomatic
Service or as a Jesuit Father you would clearly
have reached the heights. As a simple country
parson your talents are wasted. I notice with
interest that it is *I* who am charged with the task of
telling all these polite lies. Not that I blame
you—but what part do you play in this little
comedy of manners?"

There was certainly more than a suggestion of
smugness in Mr Hetherston's smile as he protested
solemnly, "Not *lies,* my lord! Surely you would not
deny the improvement in Lady Mary's spirits, nor
fail to give the credit where it is so clearly due? It is
equally true that Miss Wayburn's constant attendance on your sister renders Lady Mary less
dependent on *your* society and so does, in fact,
leave you more free to follow your own inclinations; while if those inclinations are *not* social, you
are not bound to say so. Indeed it would be sadly
ill-mannered to do so at a social gathering. I
certainly hope you will guard your tongue at the
party which my wife is giving next week and
which we hope you will honour with your presence.
Nothing grand, you know. Just a few conversable
friends to dine with perhaps a little music and a
rubber or two of whist afterwards."

They were on such famous terms by this time
that Lord Stapleford did not attempt to hide his
horror, grimacing in mock agony as he said, "I'd
be more than happy to eat my mutton with you and
Mrs. Hetherston any day of the week. But I can
guess only too accurately who your 'conversable

friends' are likely to be and the prospect terrifies me. However, if I must be sacrificed on the altar of propriety I don't see why you should have all the fun. I shall certainly invent a few ingenious tarradiddles of my own. How would it be if I were to drop a hint that I chance to be acquainted with the circumstances of Miss Wayburn's birth and find in them nothing that precludes intimacy with my sister? I daresay, you know, that she was born in much the same way as any other infant, so that is just as true as the rest. I'll lay you handsome odds that your 'conversable friends' would instantly credit me with an exact knowledge of her parentage. I have only to look sufficiently embarrassed and vow that my lips are sealed and within the sennight it would be common knowledge—known, of course, only to a few intimates—that she is the daughter of a lady of quality by one of the royal princes and that there is a strong suggestion that the pair were secretly married."

He chuckled mischievously at the Vicar's horrified face and patted him soothingly on the shoulder. "Perhaps I will not go quite so far as *that*. But I will not promise not to promote some such notion if chance offers."

Chapter 6

THE PATTERN of life at the Place changed slightly after the Vicar's morning call. Lord Stapleford announced that his pupil's progress was such that the evening lessons should now be extended to include the rest of the schoolroom party and that they might perhaps read aloud scenes from such of Shakespeare's plays as Miss Parminter thought suitable. Lissa found this much more amusing than her solitary readings but missed the intimacy of the times when she had been free to talk as she wished, to ask questions that she could not put to anyone else and to feel—and this was the nub of the matter—that his lordship enjoyed her society, shared her sense of the ridiculous and even, she ventured to think, quite *liked* her as a person, regardless of her anomalous social position.

The riding lessons continued whenever the weather permitted but apart from this they saw little of his lordship who seemed to be increasingly involved in social engagements, until Lady Mary, grown bold in her new self-confidence, charged him with desertion and wondered wistfully, but with a wicked dimple that delighted him, if he found the Wetherley girls or Lady Sophia Retford more amusing than herself and Lissa. Her brother pulled her ringlets and informed her that it was not at all the thing to beg so brazenly for compliments. He did not tell her how deadly dull he found his truly heroic efforts to undo the harm caused by his earlier casual behaviour, or how often he wished that the evening reading might be prolonged in the informal family gatherings that would preclude the need to do the polite to some haughty dowager or, worse still, to invent empty compliments for her daughters.

Admittedly there were some moments of compensation. In early December hard frost set in and the lake in the park froze. After three days his lordship decreed that it was safe for skating. Lessons were abandoned, even Miss Parminter joining in the general excitement, for this was a rare treat. Skates were hunted out and the entire party set out for the ice where they disported themselves with varying degrees of agility. Lissa, picking herself up from one of her frequent tumbles, wondered admiringly how it was that Miss Parminter managed to look even more dignified as she glided about the ice than she did on dry land, while his lordship—but perhaps one had better not refine too much on the perfection of that tall athletic figure. She was becoming increasingly aware that his lordship intruded all too often into her private thoughts.

Having tried out the ice on his family—or his

family on the ice—his lordship, deciding that his
character was now sufficiently re-established, sent
out invitations to the young folk of the
neighbourhood to attend a skating party the
following day, adding that while he knew it was
shockingly short notice, no one could foretell how
long the hard weather would last and they must
make the most of it. Since he was engaged to call
on Mrs. Wetherley, he, himself, carried the invitation to her daughters. Both young ladies were
seated with their Mama in the drawing-room when
his lordship was announced, though only Miss
Phoebe was to be regarded as really "out," the
sixteen-year-old Clarissa being still in the schoolroom. They fell at once into raptures over the
delicious scheme, begging their Mama with pretty
impulsiveness not to deny them the offered treat.
Mama, eyeing them fondly and proudly and
hoping that Lord Stapleford was properly impressed by the charming picture that they presented, arms gracefully entwined about each other's
waists, appealing faces lifted to hers, said that she
would think it over. She added, with unwonted
indulgence, that they might go and look out their
skates in case her decision was favourable. A
further appeal from Miss Clarissa having been
promptly quelled by a sharp nip from Miss Phoebe,
the sisters withdrew with becoming shy curtseys,
the whole effect rather spoiled by Miss Clarissa's
neglecting to close the door properly before
commencing to upbraid her sister in an audible
whine, vowing that her arm was already showing
the bruise.

Their mother, ignoring this slight contretemps with Olympian indifference, turned a sharply suspicious eye upon her caller. "I am sure it is very kind of you, Stapleford, to invite my little girls to share your pleasure, but I declare, I scarcely know how to answer you. With girls, you know, one cannot be too careful. I would not for the world expose them to any undesirable influence. Tell me, pray, is the Wayburn child to be of the party? One hears that she is seen everywhere with your sister, and I am not at all sure—" She allowed the sentence to trail off and looked at him searchingly.

Perhaps it was that beady inquisitive eye or the dominant, sharply curving nose, somehow suggestive of a bird of prey about to strike. At any rate his lordship allowed temptation to over-ride any scruples that he might have felt about departing from the strict truth. He smiled at his hostess quite charmingly and said, "Miss Wayburn? There is no cause for anxiety, ma'am. I think she has inherited a little of that inimitable character. She is most unassuming, quite unspoilt in spite of her birth, without the least height in her manner. Of course she has not been told the whole truth and does not realise on just how high a form she might—" He, too, allowed the sentence to trail away, with a shrug and a spreading of the hands that indicated his own superior knowledge, and then went on in encouraging tones, "So you see there is not the least need for your daughters to feel shy."

There was a brief pregnant pause while the lady sought for breath and tried to assimilate the incredible implication of Stapleford's remarks.

Then an expression of sudden anxiety erased his friendly smile and his fingers flew up to his mouth in a gesture of deep dismay.

"Oh! Good God, ma'am!" In his sudden agitation he had clearly forgotten to mind his tongue. "Never say you did not know! Indeed I never dreamed—such an old and trusted friend! Ma'am, ma'am, I throw myself on your mercy. I can only beg you to forget what I have said and never to mention it to a living soul. Believe me when I say that it would be shocking beyond belief if anything that you may have conjectured from my rash words should ever pass beyond the walls of this room. How could I have been so grossly, so criminally careless? Pray permit me to take my leave of you. I am wholly overset and must consider carefully whether I ought not at once to inform— But I beg of you once more—the utmost discretion." He made her a very flustered bow, pressed his hand to a brow presumably fevered with anxiety, and hurried out of the room still muttering to himself.

Mrs. Wetherley, for once completely shattered, uncertain what to make of the farrago of hints and half sentences that his lordship had let fall, cast herself upon a sofa and fumbled blindly on the table for a seldom used vinaigrette. After a prolonged period of reflection she decided that there were several possible solutions that would fit the puzzle he had set her, and one, in particular, that caused even so noted a connoisseur of the "on dit" to suck in her breath in reverential awe. Her difficulty was to decide upon her next move.

Should she attempt, by subtle blackmail, to coerce Stapleford into telling her the whole? Such a course sorted ill with her pride. If she could discover it for herself, she could then pretend that she had been in the secret all the time. Eventually she reached only one firm decision—that she herself would chaperone the girls to tomorrow's skating party instead of leaving that tedious task to Clarissa's governess. It was several years since she had set eyes on Wayburn girl. It was possible that now that she was almost grown up she might bear a marked resemblance to one or other of the distinguished gentlemen at whom his lordship had hinted. She would see for herself. Time enough then to decide on her further conduct.

His lordship's groom, summoned in haste from the Wetherley stables where he had been proudly holding forth to an admiring audience on the manifest perfections of the prime bits o' blood and bone that his master had chosen to drive that day, was at first at a loss to account for this change of plan. It was then borne in upon him that his lordship had been seized with a sudden illness. He seemed unable to speak clearly, his face was contorted into the strangest grimace and he actually signed to Tom to take the reins. In deep anxiety Tom wasted no time in obeying, thankful for the smooth action that would ensure the greatest possible comfort for his passenger and wondering how soon he could get him home and how long it would take to fetch the doctor from Wilton.

Alas for such misdirected sympathy! No sooner

had the lodgekeeper closed the gates of 'Peacocks' behind the curricle, even before they were safely out of sight round the bend in the road, than his lordship threw back his head, which had been sunk on his chest, and gave way to such a paroxysm of mirth that Tom actually found himself chuckling in sympathy without the least notion of the cause of the outburst. That set his master off again. He clung to the side of the curricle and rocked with laughter until he choked and the tears ran down his face. When at last the convulsion abated and he had mopped his face with a handkerchief, he suggested, in a voice still raw from excessive laughter, that Tom might put 'em along a bit, since they were not, so far as he was aware, bound for a funeral. The curricle then proceeded more briskly, his lordship still giving vent to an occasional snort of laughter as he recalled the expression on Mrs. Wetherley's face. But as they neared home he grew more subdued. The possible repercussions of his deliberate mischief began to arise in gloomy array. For himself he did not care a fig. The scrape he was in was cheap at the price. But he had been so carried away by his own histrionic talent and the ease with which he had bamboozled the old she-dragon that he had momemtarily forgotten that Lissa would once again become the target for all the gossip mongers. It was too much to hope that Mrs. Wetherley would keep such a choice morsel to herself. It was unlikely that anyone would have the effrontery to question the girl directly, but he could well imagine the turning of heads, the nods,

the nudges and the sly whispers that would attend
her simplest appearance in public. By the time
they were bowling up the avenue he was heartily
regretting his folly, and yet, at the same time,
aware of a curious desire to unfold the whole story
to the innocent victim. She might be shocked and
frightened. He thought it was far more likely that
she would thoroughly enjoy the joke. He sighed
impatiently for the impossible situation into
which he had got himself and informed his
startled groom that it was a great mistake to
partake in play readings since it was apt to give
one an exaggerated notion of one's own talents
and an irrepressible desire to display them. Tom,
who could just about manage to read those bits of
the prayer book that he knew by heart anyway,
gulped and looked sideways at his master, but
realised thankfully that no answer was expected.

His lordship was very much on the fidget as the
time for the evening reading approached, even
considering taking Miss Parminter into his confidence and asking her assistance in safeguarding
Lissa from the effects of his all to successful essay
in gull catching. When the expected knock fell on
the library door he started guiltily. But it was only
Miss Parminter who came in sedately and asked if
for once he would excuse them from the reading.
Lady Mary seemed to be starting a cold. No,
nothing serious, just a sore throat and sneezes, but
she had thought the child would be better in her
bed. And then she had begged so earnestly for
Lissa to bear her company that she had consented
to ask his indulgence for once. It was a pity that his

sister would have to miss tomorrow's gaiety, but it would not do to run the risk of a further chill. At least she would be able to watch the fun, since the schoolroom window overlooked the lake.

"What about Lissa?" asked his lordship. "Mary will not wish *her* to miss the fun."

Miss Parminter looked a little surprised. "Indeed, my lord, it is no such thing," she explained. "Lady Mary did her utmost to coax Lissa to join the other guests, but quite properly the child refused. It was tactfully done, too. No least hint that it was a matter of duty—just that she would be quite petrified if she had to face a bevy of strangers without your sister's support."

With a sudden recollection of the difficulties that he himself had created for the girl his lordship forbore to press the matter further. Indeed, on further reflection, he began to feel quite grateful for Mary's fortuitous cold, a sentiment which strengthened to fervour when he found himself next morning greeting the redoubtable Mrs. Wetherley herself. It did not need a vast amount of intelligence to guess why she had chosen to attend a simple affair which she would undoubtedly find a dead bore and the gleam in that calculating eye as she enquired for Mary was definitely warlike. His excuses sounded lamentably feeble even in his own ears, despite the fact that they were true, and it was obvious from the lady's disbelieving air that she suspected him of deliberate prevarication. Luckily for him another party of guests arrived before she could pursue the matter further and he took care thereafter to avoid her dangerous vicinity. Since she made no further effort to corner him alone, his lordship was eventually able to relax and even to enjoy the party.

He was an excellent host, noticing in a trice if anyone seemed to be left out of the fun and contriving to draw them into a congenial group without undue fuss. A good skater himself, he was even better as a partner, using his strength and skill to exhibit the lady's graceful performance so that she felt she had never skated so well before. It was a pretty sight to watch and quite a number of the estate workers and even a few folk from the village had taken advantage of a friendly arrangement by which they were allowed to use the lane that ran through the park as a short cut to the turnpike. It was surprising how many people seemed to have business in Amesbury that morning and how many of them had time to linger at such gateways as gave a clear view of the lake to watch the quality disporting themselves. The Viscount recognised a few familiar faces among the onlookers. One was Mrs. Wayburn, who would doubtless be disappointed at not seeing Lissa among the laughing youngsters. She had a stranger with her, he noticed, a slender woman dressed in black, who even at that distance had a certain air of distinction. He asked his partner if she knew who the visitor was and she was able to tell him that this was Mrs. Wayburn's new lodger, only just arrived, and understood to be a French lady, one of those poor creatures who had lost homes and loved ones during the shocking excesses of the previous year. Lord Stapleford

nodded sympathetic interest and turned the talk to
more cheerful matters.

Mrs. Wayburn, seeing that her companion
looked pinched with cold, suggested that they
should make their way home. She expressed her
regret that her foster child had not been among the
skaters and then related in voluble detail the story
of the girl's good fortune in finding such a splendid
post. The Comtesse de Valmeuse was an excellent
listener and seemed to have a remarkably good
understanding of the English language. Perhaps,
thought kindly Mrs. Wayburn, a story so romantic
and unusual as Lissa's would afford her temporary distraction from brooding over the shocking
death of her husband. "'Tis strange to think that
had I not answered Mr. Whitehead's advertisement for a home for the child, *you* would not be
here now," she ended thoughtfully. "I hope I shall
be able to make you comfortable after his recom-
mending me so high. I daresay it's not at all what
you've been used to."

If she hoped that in response to this inviting
opening the Comtesse would obligingly reveal a
little more of her own story, she was disappointed.
All she got was a courteous rejoinder that her guest
had no anxieties on that score and was grateful for
the healing peace of the countryside. She gave it
up. If the lady did not wish to talk of the past it was
ill-mannered to persist. She pointed out various
landmarks that would help the stranger to find her
way about if she should venture abroad unaccompanied.

When first Mr. Whitehead's letter had come,

asking if she would care to take in a French widow
lady who wished to live secluded in the country,
Nanty had wondered at once if the lady had
anything to do with Lissa. There was the fact of
her introduction by the same lawyer and Nanty's
own belief that the doll that had been sent to the
child was French. This was partly why she had
complied with the suggestion for she had never
taken lodgers and was not at all sure that she
wanted one now. The lawyer's letter had assured
her that the lady had funds in England and would
be able to pay an adequate sum for her accommodation, but it was that faint possibility that there
might be some connection with her fosterling—
that the lady might even be the child's own
mother—that had swayed her towards acceptance,
rather than the financial inducement. Her first
sight of the Comtesse proved disappointing. She
could trace no resemblance to Lissa in this
olive-skinned, dark-eyed lady, her black hair
showing frosted with silver beneath her widow's
cap. But now that she was there in the flesh,
Nanty's motherly heart went out to her as a
woman who had suffered tragically. She did her
utmost to make the Comtesse comfortable though
she shook her head sadly over the long hours that
the lady spent in brooding, her delicate embroidery
lying neglected in her lap. Much better if she had
some occupation to fill her mind and banish
haunting memories. It was almost a pity that she
had no need to earn her bread.

His lordship, having regaled his guests at an
informal and extremely noisy nuncheon, waved

farewell to the last departing carriage and turned back to the house, thankful to have the morning safely over without being plunged more deeply in the morass of deceit. An imperative tapping on the windowpane drew his attention to two heads in the schoolroom window. There was Mary, waving and beckoning, and Lissa standing a little behind the shorter girl. He would go up and tell them all about the party he decided, with an inexplicable lifting of his spirits. They had had a dull day of it. On a sudden inspiration he collected from the silent drawing-room a certain well-worn mahogany box which had beguiled many a lonely hour in his own childhood. A flowing inscription on the inside of the lid described it as "A Compleat Compendium of Games of Skill," and in addition to a set of finely carved chessmen, draughts and playing cards, it also held more frivolous things, among them a set of Jackstraws.

It was an afternoon that would always stay vivid in Lissa's memory. She had not really minded missing the skating; had even been relieved rather than otherwise. On the previous day she had spent far more time in picking herself up and starting all over again than in gliding gracefully over the ice. She got on well enough as long as she pushed a chair in front of her but as soon as she abandoned this support, down she went. It hadn't mattered a bit, even when they all laughed at her, for they were her friends. But she had no particular desire to be a laughing stock for strangers, many of whom, she guessed, would be well pleased to poke malicious fun at her deficien-

cies. Mary and she had enjoyed a good view of the
proceedings from the schoolroom window and she
had noticed that his lordship did not skate more
than once with any of his partners, not even with
the pretty Lady Sophia who skated so beautifully
and whose big blue eyes and golden curls con-
trasted so charmingly with his lordship's almost
Spanish darkness. No doubt this was just his
notion of the conduct proper from a host to his
guests, but somehow it assuaged an unidentified
anxiety that lay hidden in her heart. Moreover his
face had lit with genuine pleasure at Mary's urgent
signals and he had wasted no time in joining them
in the schoolroom. After that the hours had passed
all too swiftly. Perhaps it was the schoolroom
atmosphere that made his lordship seem suddenly
young and carefree—no longer the important and
potentially frightening arbiter of her destiny.
Perhaps it was just the foolish games that they
played and the blatant way in which he cheated at
Jackstraws, loudly declaring that it was Mary's
sneeze that had shaken the intricately balanced
pile, never *his* expert and delicate touch. Miss
Parminter, who had declared herself too old for
such childish pastimes, beamed on the three of
them with warm approval and, for the first time in
her life, reflected that her lot had been cast in
pleasant places.

When Janet brought up schoolroom tea his
lordship insisted on staying to share it and
demanded bread to toast over the fire and cherry
jam and plum cake, though it might have been
noticed that he partook very sparingly of these

delicacies when a smiling Janet produced them, appointing himself toaster-in-chief and keeping the girls in a ripple of merriment by his objurgatory remarks addressed to such pieces of bread as scorched or fell off the fork. Replete with toast and laughter they finally assured him that they could not swallow another crumb and sat lazily in the firelight talking of plans for the Christmas holiday while Miss Parminter worked industriously at the embroidery of the slippers that she proposed to present to her great-uncle as a Christmas gift. His lordship, toying idly with the scattered Jackstraws, told them stories of his childhood and how he had built forts with the nursery blocks, defended them with armies of chessmen and draughts and attacked them with toy soldiers armed with Jackstraws, even pointing out the brown mark on one ivory sliver, a spear, which, hurled with excessive energy, had gone straight into the nursery fire and been retrieved by a frightened small boy at the cost of blistered fingers.

He glanced up at the end of this woeful tale to see Lissa's great eyes fixed upon him with such an expression of sorrowful sympathy that he felt quite uncomfortable and lowered his gaze to the littered table, suggesting that a pair of idle useless brats would be better employed in tidying up the games box. It did not occur to him that Lissa's sympathy had not been for the blisters but for a lonely little boy making his own amusements without even a loving Nanty to share his joys and comfort his childish sorrows. It was as bad as being an unwanted love-child. For the first time she realised that wealth and noble birth did not always bring happiness and in the realisation took another step towards maturity.

Chapter 7

AFTER ALL their plans and joyous anticipation the Christmas holiday turned out to be sadly flat. Ten days before the festival his lordship received an imperious summons to present himself at Wrelf, where the Marquis was entertaining a large party for the better part of a month. It was a summons impossible to refuse, for beneath the reproaches for recent neglect and the acid comments on the total lack of gratitude and respect in the younger generation was plain to be read an old man's loneliness, his desire for a reconciliation with his heir. They had parted in coldness; the rare letters they had exchanged had been formal and, in the main, concerned with estate business. The Marquis would never stoop to plead—he spoke only of the advisability of meeting some of Society's leaders at Wrelf, where the boy would be at an advantage in the delicate business of re-establishing himself in the eyes of the polite world. Lord Stapleford sighed. He was rather weary of this business of making himself acceptable to his

89

neighbours. It would make a pleasant change, he felt, if someone actually approved of him when he was his natural self! First Hetherston and now his grandfather, telling him how he should go on. The Marquis expounded on this theme at length, explaining just how he should set about making himself agreeable to the various notabilities whom he might expect to meet, and offering as an inducement the prospect that success would shorten his banishment. His lordship, who was finding himself singularly well content with country life, sighed resignedly and sat down to write his reply, promising to present himself at Wrelf on the Tuesday before Christmas if road conditions permitted.

This change of plan cast a deep glow over the schoolroom. Neither coaxing nor teasing nor the promise of a truly magnificent Christmas gift when he returned could bring back the smiles to Mary's woebegone little face, though she did brighten a little at his promise of an early return and his reminder that at least, this year, she would have Lissa to keep her company. "But it won't be the same if you're not here," she said sadly. "And we had planned all sorts of surprises for you."

"And I refuse to be cheated out of them," said her brother. "Promise you'll save them all for when I come back and we'll keep our own holiday then."

Christmas did however bring them a new acquaintance, one whom both girls and governess found attractive and entertaining. Mrs. Wayburn's lodger accompanied her hostess to church on Christmas Day, to the surprise of those

who had automatically assumed her to be of the
Roman Catholic persuasion, and it was natural for
the two parties to walk home together. Miss
Parminter's relations with her two charges had
mellowed considerably of late and she was sincerely sorry for them in their disappointment over
his lordship's absence, so she raised no objection
when Nanty invited them to step inside for a few
moments and taste her home-brewed mead and her
mince pies. Since the Comtesse was also invited to
share this seasonable hospitality the three older
ladies chatted in friendly fashion while Lissa
begged permission to show Lady Mary the tiny
attic room that was still "hers" and the childish
treasures that Nanty guarded for her. Presently
Nanty excused herself to attend to the progress of
dinner which had been left to its own devices while
they were at church.

The Comtesse de Valmeuse had been famed for
her social address even at a court that was
renowned for its polished courtesy. She found no
difficulty in providing a flow of polite small talk.
But her gentle commonplaces were met with an
interest that they scarcely merited and she
realised that here was a shy and lonely woman,
eager for colour and warmth and friendship.
Deliberately she set herself to draw out the
cramped butterfly spirit which she believed to
exist in any feminine breast, however unpromis-
ing the exterior. Before long the unlikely pair had
discovered several mutual interests and prejudices
and were deep in talk when Nanty came back
flushed and apologetic for her long absence. The

sliding "cheek" which controlled the heat of the
oven had jammed and she had been struggling to
release it. However all was well and the beef was
not scorched but dinner would be slightly delayed.

Upon hearing this Madame de Valmeuse said
that she would walk a little way with her new
acquaintance. Mrs. Wayburn was intrigued to
hear her add, "And I will look out my sketch book
and bring it with me on Thursday," as she turned
to her hostess and said pleasantly, with scarcely a
trace of foreign accent, "Miss Parminter assures
me that you will consent to act as my guide to the
Place on that occasion as you will be making your
weekly visit and she has very kindly invited me to
take tea with her."

The newborn friendship flourished, until there
were few days when "Madame," as she preferred to
be called, did not make her way up to the Place at
some time of the day, either to talk to the girls in
French or Italian, or to supervise their painting,
for Miss Parminter had found her to be an
extremely talented artist. She herself, though
well-taught was quite devoid of talent and was
delighted that her pupils should have the advantage of seeing such beautiful work. She did demur
at having Madame take over tasks that were
rightly hers but was laughed to scorn by that lady
who declared that she would soon have been
moped to death if it had not been for the pleasant
society that she found at the Place. So schoolroom
life went on very comfortably though it lacked the
gaiety that the Viscount had brought to it.

That gentleman was, indeed, much more moped

and bored than the cosy quartet at Stapleford. To
Wrelf itself he was devoted. But it was the country
way of life that he loved, and he saw his home
neither as a decorative background for spoilt
society beauties nor as a select club for gamesters
and dandies. And that, in his present disgruntled
frame of mind, was how he felt his grandfather's
guests used it. Who wanted to lie in bed till noon
when the moors were crisp with frost and there
were birds a-plenty and only a week or two of the
season left? Or spend the evenings in insipid
exchanges with debutantes who knew no better
than to agree with everything one said? A few
months out of Town, he discovered, and half the
conversation was unintelligible. He did not know
the latest crim. cons. nor care who had fathered the
Betterston twins. Even the hints of political
intrigue aimed at bringing down Pitt sounded like
backstairs gossip, unworthy of serious consideration. The ladies found him poor company. His
grandfather, though the pair were good friends
again, was sadly disappointed because he had not
fallen a victim to one of the delectable trio of fillies
whom he had specially selected for his grandson to
look over. It was full time that the boy got over his
foolish fancy for Millicent Girling and since that
enchantress had been the darkest of brunettes the
Marquis had congratulated himself on choosing
two blondes and a chestnut, all of impeccable
pedigree and all nicely broken to bridle, as he
phrased it to himself. Jervase was perfectly
charming to all of them, but not even Sylvia
Dysart's ethereal fairness and the pretty little lisp

that Society had pronounced to be so attractive that its owner now practised it assiduously in private as well as in public, had succeeded in earning her any distinguishing attentions from the impervious Viscount. Had the Marquis but known it, his grandson considered that the lady stood in dire need of lessons in speaking without ridiculous affectation, though he felt no inclination to attend to the matter himself. As for Lady Genevra's much admired auburn locks, he thought they probably owed a good deal to the skilled use of the dye pot since she certainly had not the temperament to go with them. They compared very unfavourably with some red-gold curls with which he was well acquainted and in comparing the two and remembering how Lissa Wayburn's hair shone guinea gold at her brow and temples his lordship suffered such a pang of homesickness for Stapleford that he suggested to his grandfather that he should take his departure with the rest of the house party.

The Marquis would not hear of it. With the house so full of people there had been no opportunity for a comfortable talk with the boy. He wanted to hear how he went on at Stapleford and what he planned to do, now that the way seemed reasonably clear for his return to Town. When the guests were gone they would have opportunity to discuss such topics at length. The Viscount could think of nothing that he would like less. Uneasily aware that the less his grandfather knew about certain of his doings at Stapleford, especially those that concerned his old friend, Mrs. Wetherley, the better it

would be for their newly restored amity, and
finding that he regarded the prospect of an early
return to Town with inexplicable distaste, he
evaded as best he could and renewed his suggestion of an early departure, pointing out that once
February was in there would be little to do at Wrelf.

"Does not Stapleford suffer from the same
disadvantages, then?" enquired the Marquis
dryly. "I begin to suspect that it must hold some
hidden attraction."

He knew from the letters of friends that the boy
had shut himself away for weeks but of late had
seemed to be emerging from his self-imposed
seclusion. That was perfectly natural. His comment had been the merest jest. But when Stapleford coloured up and denied the idle imputation
with quite unnecessary heat he began to think
there might be something in it.

"You protest too much, my boy," he grinned.
"Never tell me that Galahad has found himself a
rustic charmer after all!"

But Jervase had recovered from the accidental
hit. "Rating me too high, Sir," he said lazily,
returning the grin. "I was never a Galahad.
Good-looking sort of cove, wasn't he? All the ladies
after him? Bit of a slow-top though. Brought up by
nuns, if my memory serves me. Accounts for it.
Couldn't expect a lot of spinsters, however holy, to
understand bringing up a boy. I did find myself a
pretty little charmer, though. Her name is Mary
and she will be fifteen next month. What's more I
found her in much the same sad case as poor old
Galahad, for that governess you selected for her is

as near to being a nun as makes no odds."

The amusement vanished from his grandfather's face to be replaced by a scowl. "What sort of a female do you expect a governess to be?" he demanded, instantly resenting the first breath of criticism. "Would you have me employ one who was *not* of the highest respectability to instruct your sister?" And then, with dawning interest, "So Mary's growing into a beauty, is she? Scarce surprising. Your mother was the toast of the Town. Is she better in health? I think of her still as a puny sickly brat. But close on fifteen! I must soon began to look about for a good match for her."

Jervase hastened to correct these impressions. "No, Sir, not a beauty, though she has considerable charm and is neither puny nor sickly. Nor is she anywhere near marriage ripe. I thought she was being kept too close to her books and I know you have no liking for scholarly women so I made a few changes. I've been teaching her to ride and have engaged a caper merchant to instruct her in the elegancies of the dance. And I have found a companion for her, a child of her own age to share her lessons and encourage her in a little harmless mischief. I promise you, Sir, the change in my meek little mouse of a sister is a vast improvement."

The Marquis grunted sourly, not sure that he approved this flagrant interference with the arrangements that were *his* province but unable to find grounds for complaint in the boy's kindly interest in his sister's welfare. Then he pounced on the weak spot.

"Who's this companion wench?" he demanded suspiciously. "Why did you bring in a stranger? Why not one of the Goldsborough brats if companionship was needed?"

"Lissa Wayburn, Sir?" said Jervase smoothly, though with a silent prayer for inspiration which he addressed rather to the Reverend Michael Hetherston than to the Almighty. "I doubt if you are acquainted with Mrs. Wayburn. She is not one of our tenants. Widow of a naval man. Straitened means, I imagine—ekes out a living with her needle. The Vicar had interested himself in the child and taken her education in hand, but she was too much with the village children and was growing slovenly in her speech. It seemed to me a good scheme, though I confess I might have thought of the Goldsborough cousins. Mrs. Wayburn feels herself much obliged to us, Mary likes the girl and Miss Parminter, who was doubtful at the outset, is now wholly in agreement."

And that last statement, at least, was a whole truth, he thought thankfully, with a sudden determination that once he was clear of the present entanglement he would, in future, shun prevarication as he would the devil. It might be amusing when you used it to fool a shrew like Mrs. Wetherley, but it was mean and despicable to use his grandfather so. Tyrant and tartar he might be, but he had always shown great kindness to his grandson. Yet what else could he do, since it was not his own comfort that was at stake but a girl's reputation. Let the Marquis but set eyes on Lissa and there was only one interpretation that he would put upon the circumstances.

The Marquis grunted, only half satisfied by the explanation, admonishing his heir that it would not do to let his revolutionary notions cause him to cherish any stray brat that touched his pity, and enquired more particularly into the rank and career of the late Mr. Wayburn. Jervase was thankful that he could truthfully plead ignorance. He then submitted meekly to a sharp tongue lashing for having neglected to discover these important details before permitting the girl to associate with his sister. The interview left him feeling so shamefully guilty that he found it quite impossible to refuse his grandfather's request that he should stay on at Wrelf until the Marquis's own return to Town so that they might travel together.

Thus it was that February was already a week old when he rode into the stable yard at the Place, quite unheralded, at close upon nine o'clock one night. He had meant to lie at Salisbury, but the combination of dry weather, a bright moon and the proximity of home was too tempting. He instructed Tom to bring on the chaise and the baggage next day, hired a tidy hack and pushed on without waiting for dinner.

At that hour of the night the house was almost entirely in darkness. Most of the servants would be already abed. A startled footman admitted him and went to take order for his master's reception. The Viscount, having noted that one of the few lights that broke the dark frontage came from Miss Parminter's sitting-room, decided that he would drop in on the lady to ascertain that all had gone well during his absence and took the stairs two at a time to tap politely on her door. A rather surprised voice bidding him enter, he opened the door on an unexpected scene.

There were three people in the room instead of the one he had thought to see. Miss Parminter had risen from her chair by the fire and was expressing her surprise and gratification at seeing him. He scarcely heard her. Standing with her back to him, working intently on a painting that stood on an easel, was a stranger, a woman dressed in black, who did not even look up until Miss Parminter greeted him by name. Then she turned to gaze at him, the brush suspended in her hand, her expression cool and critical, her poise untouched by his sudden irruption into the quiet room. Beyond recording the fact that she was a stranger he paid little heed to her, either. All his attention was for Lissa; Lissa, who should have been in bed this half-hour past; a Lissa who was almost a stranger, wearing a close fitting green velvet riding dress and a beaver hat with sweeping plumes in the fashion of yester year, a riding crop in her gloved hand.

For a moment he did not grasp the simple and obvious explanation that the stranger was painting Lissa's portrait. He simply wondered, rather stupidly, why she was so oddly dressed at this hour of the night. Then she abandoned her pose, ran across the room to greet him and sank into a deep graceful curtsey, her face joyful, her eyes glowing with a light that was frankly adoring.

Miss Parminter made a mental note to remind

her pupil that so profound a reverence was not appropriate to his lordship's rank, but did not see the rapt look on her face. Nor did Madame, whose attention was for the newcomer.

She saw him check suddenly, as one who had received a shock. For a brief moment it was difficult to read his expression. Then he was smiling at Lissa and bowing deeply in return for her greeting, giving his hand to help her rise and conducting her with some ceremony to the chair on which her free hand had been posed when he interrupted the sitting. He then suggested, with a teasing twinkle, that it was rather unusual to perform a court curtsey with a whip in one's hand and left the recipient in some doubt as to one's ultimate intentions. Lissa laughed at that one, assured him that he stood in no immediate danger, and demanded to know if her curtsey had improved.

"Importunate brat," said his lordship. "My praise is not so lightly bestowed. Riding dress, however fine," and he studied it through his glass with some attention, "is not the proper attire for it. We shall see how you perform in full fig. There must be plenty of ancient finery laid away in the attic to furnish you with a practice dress. Meanwhile you are forgetting more immediate matters. You have not presented me to your guest."

Lissa blushed and apologised, but quite without that air of painful humiliation which had acknowledged her earlier social ineptitudes. "Madame will forgive me," she said gaily. "She knows how much we have all missed you and will understand that every other thought was forgotten when I saw you so unexpectedly returned," and performed the necessary courtesies with easy grace, adding that Madame La Comtesse had coaxed Miss Parminter to allow her to stay up a little longer than usual in order that she might use her as a model, and that the lovely riding dress was Madame's own, that she had worn as a girl, and was it not much prettier than the modern fashions?

Miss Parminter, who had watched this interlude with an indulgent eye agreed that this was true, but perhaps Lissa had better run along to bed now that the sitting was done and that she was on no account to wake Mary, who would not sleep another wink if she heard that her brother was returned. Lissa went off without demur and the Viscount was interested to see that she bestowed a good night kiss upon her friends as she bade them good night. He himself was awarded only a mischievous parody of a curtsey, a wobbling, awkward bob, eyes and mouth wide open, finger to mouth and a wicked dimple lurking. He acknowledged it appropriately with a haughty sneer and a curl of the lip that should have set her quite beneath his notice but which only evoked a deep gurgle of merriment. Things had certainly changed in his household during his absence.

With Lissa gone it was possible to converse seriously. Miss Parminter told him briefly of the Comtesse's situation and of how they had chanced to become acquainted. She spoke of her obligation to the lady for her friendship and for her help with the girls. His lordship, who had assessed the lady's

quality at a glance once his attention was no
longer absorbed by Lissa, expressed his gratitude
with patent sincerity and added that he found
Lissa improved out of recognition. Both ladies
looked pleased. "She has tried so hard," said Miss
Parminter. "She has breeding," amended the
Comtesse. "She knows instinctively what is sound
and what is cheap and tawdry."

The talk turned to painting. The Comtesse
hoped that she might be permitted to finish the
portrait and undertook to see that the sittings did
not interfere with lessons. The Viscount reminded
Miss Parminter that he had promised the girls a
holiday when he came home which would allow
plenty of time for the artist. He was not allowed to
look at the portrait which, the Comtesse said, was
scarce begun. He should see it when it was
finished. He commended her choice of costume and
Miss Parminter agreed enthusiastically that nothing could better become the child. Style and colour
alike were calculated to bring out her unusual
quality. Only the Viscount found it a little
surprising that a Frenchwoman who had, admittedly, escaped from her own country by the
narrowest of margins, should have been able to
bring with her a riding habit which she must have
discarded twenty years ago.

Chapter 8

JERVASE HAD spent most of the past five days in travelling, at a season of the year when even the hardiest avoided the roads. Yet when he bade the Comtesse and Miss Parminter a courteous good night he did not at once seek his bed. Nor did he do anything like justice to the palatable viands that had been hurriedly assembled and set out for his enjoyment in the library. He carved himself some slices of cold beef which he made into substantial sandwiches and prowled up and down the floor devouring them in absent-minded gulps. The edge of his ravening hunger thus blunted, he forgot all about it but continued his restless pacing until, suddenly aware of physical weariness, he flung himself into a chair, put his elbows on his knees and buried his face in his hands.

With his eyes closed he could see even more clearly the glorified face of the girl who had looked up at him in adoring surrender. He knew that he wanted her for his wife above anything else that the world could hold. And she was still a child, her

devotion innocent of all trace of passion. She loved
him because she saw him as a very figure of
romance, a Cophetua who had stooped to raise a
beggar child to the steps of his throne. There was
no reality in such love. It was the stuff that dreams
were made of and would never survive the touch of
harsh reality. But if he guarded her carefully, left
her free to grow into a woman and wooed her
delicately the while, might it not be that she would
learn to love him as he so deeply desired? Not as a
dream prince, but as a man—warm—faulty—
human.

Hetherston had certainly been in the right of it
about the rashness of his impulsive offer. Had he,
Jervase wondered, foreseen this particular outcome? The difficulties that beset his path seemed
mountainous. As if it were not enough that he must
wait for his little love to grow up, his grandfather
would never consent to such a marriage. It would
go sorely against the pluck to break with the old
man who had been so good to him in his own
fashion. Moreover it would mean saying good-bye
to Wrelf and Stapleford, for the Marquis would
assuredly disinherit him and he would never be
able to keep up even Stapleford, let alone Wrelf, on
the modest fortune that he had inherited from his
mother. A high-sounding title was a pretty hollow
bauble when you could not afford the style of living
that went with it. And Lissa loved the Place. If he
had to give it up, would she still care to marry him?
The dark head came up proudly, confidently. If he
could teach her to love him she would marry him
despite his poverty. Her capacity for loving was

writ clear in the generous mouth, the candid
adoring eyes; was shown in the affection that she
poured out on Mary and now, it seemed, on so
unlikely a person as Miss Parminter. A world in
which that love was freely given to himself seemed
almost too good to be true, but with all his heart he
was determined to attain it. Meanwhile he must
keep his own counsel and cherish his darling so
unobtrusively that no one, least of all Lissa
herself, should guess his secret. It was a very
serious, resolute young man who went thoughtfully up the shallow curving staircase to his bed, to
fall instantly, dreamlessly asleep.

There was joyous excitement next morning
when the baggage arrived and his lordship
presented his belated Christmas gifts. He had been
sorely puzzled to know what to buy for he had been
determined that the two girls should have matching presents. Yet because Lissa was *not* his sister
so many gifts that he would have liked to choose
were not permissible. Then he had remembered the
cold little hands that had been clasped in his as
they skated together and bought muffs, soft, silky,
white fur for Mary, black for Lissa, since all the
browns and golds seemed dull and faded beside his
memory of her hair. He had bought gloves for Miss
Parminter, of a skin so supple and a workmanship
so exquisite that it seemed suspiciously probable
that they were of French origin. Miss Parminter,
who had never received anything so elegant in her
life, laid them away in a drawer, still wrapped in
their tissue paper, refreshing her feminine soul
with an occasional peep. She would never have

dreamed of wearing them if their donor had not enquired anxiously as to whether they were the wrong size. Upon this she was eventually persuaded to wear them on Sundays to church, if the day was fine, where she vastly disconcerted Mr. Hetherston by keeping her gaze fixed on the hands lying clasped in her lap instead of on his face as had been her wont. Had he guessed the reason he would certainly have felt called upon to preach that threatened sermon on vanity.

Now that his lordship was returned the short dark days of February passed cheerfully enough. Though he had suggested a holiday the girls preferred to spend most of their mornings in the schoolroom unless it chanced to be fine enough for them to ride with him on his estate business. The village folk grew quite accustomed to seeing the little party trotting gaily by, Mary still preferring the quietest horses but much more confident than of yore, Lissa, if not straitly forbidden, inclined to attempt feats that were beyond her limited experience. His lordship was more often at home than in the weeks before Christmas, catching up, he blandly assured them, on neglected duties, though duty did not seem to prevent him from spending a good deal of his time in devising amusement for the girls.

When they were snow-bound for a week they raided the attics and two stalwart footmen laboured downstairs under trunks crammed with the discarded finery of the ages. The girls must dress up, of course, but that was not enough for his lordship. They must also assume the manners and characters of the original wearers. One or two of the costumes could be matched with the portraits in the gallery but there were some hilarious guesses at the age and ownership of others. Mary looked quite bewitching in a riding jacket of fawn worsted with a collar of matching velvet, the facings of pink silk, the buttons silver. It was cut in a very masculine style with a deeply pleated skirt and large military pockets. But her attempts at managing the hooped petticoat that went with it made her audience rock with laughter and wonder what would happen if she actually wore it on horseback, since she could not even walk across the room without a most improper display of ankle, while an attempt to seat herself with the dignity required of a Viscountess Stapleford reduced her brother to helpless mirth and caused Miss Parminter to blush with confusion and prim up her lips in a fashion that they had not seen for weeks. Sobriety was only restored when Lissa held out a tiny garment that could only have been worn by a child of two or three and asked in puzzled fashion what it was. It was an iron corset, said Miss Parminter gravely, and in the ignorance of bygone days small children had been put into such dreadful contraptions in the belief that their bodies would grow straight. The girls looked at it in horrified awe and were thankful that they lived in modern times when such abominations were no more.

Happily, at this time, they were spared the attentions of Mrs. Wetherley. Miss Phoebe had succeeded in attaching a very eligible suitor, a

gentleman of respectable fortune and extremely
nice in all matters of good ton. What was more he
was the second son of an Earl and his elder brother
was not only unmarried but was known to be of a
sickly constitution. Miss Phoebe, making no
objection to spindly legs, protruding teeth and a
chin that receded into the top fold of a beautifully
tied cravat, was all compliance and her Mama was
bending all her energies to the task of bringing this
promising fish safely to grass. She had abandoned
hope of securing Stapleford when he had lingered
so long at Wrelf, and if the Fates were kind might
yet see her daughter a Countess. The matter of
Lissa Wayburn's parentage must wait upon more
urgent affairs.

Yet despite all the fun and laughter that once
again filled the Place, matters were not just as they
had been before Christmas. For all the light-
hearted nonsense with which his lordship imbued
their pastimes there were moments when a close
observer might have perceived the serious air that
underlay the frivolity. And though he occasionally
indulged in a tussle with Mary, rumpling her hair
or teasingly holding her wrists when she
threatened physical violence in revenge for some
impudent quip, he never adopted this brotherly
attitude with Lissa. And very proper, too, approved Miss Parminter, commending his instinc-
tive good sense. The child was growing up fast and
it seemed probable that she had the passionate
and romantic nature that went with her glowing
hair and that wide, beautifully cut mouth. It was
very natural that she should worship his lordship

to the point of idolatry, so good as he had been to her. There was no harm in *that*. But it would never do for her to fall in love with him. It could not be long, now, before he returned to his proper sphere and then that particular danger would be averted. Meanwhile, his grave courtesy, his instant attention to the girl's smallest need, from the moving of a candle so that she might see better to the placing of a fire screen so that the flames should not scorch her cheeks, and his unfailing patience with her endless questions and her occasional naïve mistakes were a perfect example of the behaviour of a very great gentleman, and Miss Parminter felt that her charges were indeed fortunate to have such a standard to form their budding tastes.

That Lissa might fall in love with his lordship she could well envisage. The one danger that never entered her head was that his lordship might fall in love with Lissa. He, at least, must be well aware that such an unequal match was out of the question and would undoubtedly drop the handkerchief, when it pleased him, to some demure damsel of impeccable lineage. Olivia—for by now she and the Comtesse were on familiar terms— might shake her head and utter ominous warnings about the dangers of propinquity, but however much the pair were in each other's company they were never alone and nothing passed between them that all the world might not hear. Miss Parminter dismissed her faint uneasiness and decided that Olivia was imagining things.

So matters went on very comfortably on the surface. The Comtesse became so much a part of the familiar routine that it was difficult to imagine how they had ever managed without her. Lord Stapleford had felt some misgivings over accepting her help with the girls, help which was quite invaluable since she supplied the background of a woman experienced in both court and social life, such an atmosphere as his mother would have provided for her daughter. He knew that any offer of payment would be hurtful, even insulting, so it was fortunate that it did not seem to be necessary. The Comtesse, unlike the majority of her fellow emigrés, showed no signs of poverty. He salved his conscience by giving orders that Mrs. Wayburn should be supplied with all the dairy produce that she and her lodger could possibly require from the Home Farm and such fruits and vegetables as were available at that season. For the time being the Comtesse seemed to have abandoned Lissa's portrait and was indulging a wicked talent for caricature which respected no one, from his lordship's ponderous butler to his lordship's self, and was appreciated even by its victims.

With the coming of spring their little community flourished in increasing isolation as one after another the local gentry returned to Town to open up their houses for the Season. Save for asking Miss Parminter to see that the girls had new gowns, appropriate to the promise of warmer weather, the Viscount seemed unaware of the passage of time and showed no sign of planning to return to Town himself.

Instead it was Miss Parminter who was quite

unexpectedly called upon to do so. The daffodils were spreading their golden frills about the hems of the great house when a middle aged manservant cantered up the drive one afternoon demanding speech with her. She had some difficulty in recognising him, since he had but newly taken service with her Great-uncle Carnforth when she had bidden farewell to that sombre establishment in Bloomsbury some twelve years ago, but he was able to identify himself to her satisfaction. He was come, he explained soberly, to summon her to his master's deathbed. She was the sole surviving creature linked to him by ties of blood and he had taken a fancy to have her in attendance on his passing.

The nature of General Carnforth's illness was somewhat obscure. He had always been of a full and bronchial habit and had found the spring weather treacherous. This year, an unusually severe attack following close upon a sharp set-to with influenza had persuaded him that he was booked and he had despatched Dawber to escort his great-niece to London, not omitting a pithy reminder that she need not expect a comfortable inheritance upon his demise. She had already had all the good she was like to get of him and his bones would make meagre picking, but if she had any sense of family obligation, etc., etc. Dawber softened the message as best he could since he dare not for his life omit it. For one supposedly moribund the cantankerous old devil had been amazingly fluent and precise. In fact, so ill prepared for heaven was he that it would not at all surprise Dawber if a stay of execution were granted.

Miss Parminter heard him out with admirable calm and consented to accompany him back to Town. The day and hour must depend on what temporary arrangements his lordship could make to fill her place but she felt that a simple solution was ready to hand and anticipated little delay. His lordship, strolling up from the stables, met the news of the impending disruption of his household with equanimity until he remembered Lissa. He expressed proper concern for Miss Parminter's aged relative and said that of course she must go to him at once; added carelessly that it would do Mary no harm to take a brief holiday—and then stopped short. "But what about Lissa?" he demanded urgently. "She cannot remain under my roof unchaperoned."

Somewhere in the depths of Miss Parminter's awareness an alarm was sounded. His lordship was too instantly concerned for a matter that should have been the merest afterthought. If no suitable arrangement could be made, Lissa could perfectly well go home for a few weeks. There was no occasion to devote such anxious attention to so small a matter, even to accomplishing the ruin of a beautifully tied cravat by tugging abstractedly at its folds while he wrestled with the problem. She said, rather repressively, "As to that, my lord, if the notion meets with your approval, I had thought that the Comtesse de Valmeuse might be persuaded to take my place for a little while; just until I can see for myself how matters stand with my uncle."

His instant acquiescence was perhaps natural under the circumstances, but surely the relief and delight that he expressed were a little excessive? Her eyes suddenly opened to a danger that she had not anticipated, Miss Parminter mentally resolved to have a serious talk with Lissa before she took her departure.

She found it uncommonly difficult. The child was so absurdly innocent that hinting was of no avail. And to make the task even more awkward she was really not quite sure what it was that she feared. She sensed that his lordship was more interested in the girl than was wise or proper, but could not credit him with a deliberate attempt at seduction. If Lissa were to become aware of that interest she might well respond with an ardour that could sweep the pair of them into dangerous waters. Yet to warn the girl might precipitate the very crisis that she feared. She compromised by asking her to be particularly circumspect during her absence, saying that now she was almost grown up she must no longer expect the licence that was granted to a child. Lissa looked puzzled and distressed and asked at once if she had transgressed in any way. Poor Miss Parminter sighed and tried to explain. "It is just that your situation is of particular delicacy. I wish that I had not to leave you just now. You are devoted to his lordship I know, and seeing so much of him and his manners so free—not that he would ever go beyond the line—in short, my dear, it would not be at all

strange if you were to fancy yourself in love with
him. Girls of your age are prone to such romantical
attachments. And I need not tell you that it would
never do, for you are a sensible child, but I felt I
should just drop a word in your ear. Nothing but
heartache could come of it."

She felt uneasily that she had already said too
much for Lissa was gazing at her with eyes grown
huge and pansy dark, as one stunned by some
strange new vision, unsure as yet whether it
promised good or ill, and even as she uttered her
final warning a wave of colour flushed the delicate
skin and the girl turned her head away from the
anxious gaze. But after a moment or two she spoke,
quietly enough.

"It was kind in you to think of me, and to warn
me, dear Miss Parminter. But I think I stand in
little danger. It is true that I love his lordship with
my whole heart, but that brings me happiness, not
heartache. My only wish is to serve him, and that I
may do by helping his sister. I could never imagine
myself 'in love' with him. It would seem—oh, I do
not know how to say it—an impertinence, I think.
A nameless waif daring to raise her eyes so high."
And then she shocked her preceptress to the core
by adding wistfully, "It's not as though I were
pretty. He wouldn't even want me as his mistress."

"Good heavens, child! Never speak so again!
Such thoughts should never enter your head, far
less pass your lips. His lordship is by far too great a
gentleman to nourish any such evil design, and
you, I must pray, will learn to value yourself better.
You have health and ability and good fortune as

well, in that you are receiving a fine education to give you a start in life. You may reasonably hope to secure an eligible situation and perhaps in the fullness of time you may marry respectably. But *not* if you give utterance to such shocking sentiments! Meanwhile, here is my direction in Bloomsbury. Write and tell me how you all go on, for I daresay I shall be sadly homesick. And remember, child, I am your true friend. If ever you need help I shall be happy to serve you." And Lissa hugged her and thanked her and apologised all in one breath so that she seemed a veritable child once more, and Miss Parminter was a little comforted.

Chapter 9

BECAUSE SHE had grown up in the village, Lissa was accustomed to a greater degree of freedom than was usually permitted to a young lady. It never occurred to her to ask anyone's permission when she wished to stroll abroad, far less to request the proper chaperonage of maid or companion on her excursions. And since she and Mary were almost inseparable and she had never chanced to go beyond the limits of the estate unaccompanied the wisdom of such behaviour had never been called in question.

On this particular Thursday afternoon, however, Mary was fully occupied with fittings for the new dresses that Miss Parminter had ordered, a proceeding which, she gloomily prophesied, was like to take up most of the afternoon, with Madame so very particular about the cut of a sleeve or the set of a skirt, and unwilling to let the dressmaker depart until her meticulous standards were satisfied.

Nanty had been confined to the house for

several days with sharp attack of rheumatism,
unable, for once, to fulfil her regular engagement
at the Place. Knowing how much she would miss
this high treat of her week, Lissa decided to run
down to the village to see her while Mary was busy
with Miss Kemble. There could be no danger of
carrying any infection back to her delicate friend
since rheumatism was not catching, and no other
consideration occurred to her.

The afternoon was one of April's loveliest and
her visit was a great success. She found Nanty
much recovered, smiling in the warmth of the
gentle sunlight and delighted to hear all the
snippets of information from the big house, from
the colours of the new spring dresses to the great
kindness that the Comtesse used towards her two
charges and the latest news in the letter that Lissa
had received from Miss Parminter. No definite
date was fixed as yet for that lady's return, though
it now seemed likely that General Carnforth would
recover to plague his servants for some time yet.
His outspoken criticism of the conduct of the war,
in particular of the pitiful inadequacy of the force
that had been dispatched to the Low Countries to
reinforce the Dutch in the defence of their frontiers
had been triumphantly vindicated, and this had
exercised a revivifying effect on his spirits. His
physician, more exhausted than the patient, had
hopefully suggested a course of the waters at
Tunbridge Wells, or better still—since it was
further from Town—at Bath, but no decision had
yet been reached as to which of these salubrious
spots should be so honoured.

All these details were meat and drink to Mrs. Wayburn who waved a beaming farewell from the doorway and reiterated that it would not be necessary for Lissa to visit her the following Thursday since she was sure to be well enough to resume her usual habits. Time had passed more quickly than Lissa had realised and she hastened her steps, wishing to pick a posy of the primroses that she had noticed growing in sheltered spots under the hedge on her way down the lane. Madame had expressed a liking for the delicate blossoms and these were the first that Lissa had seen. So she hurried past the Church and the parsonage, only to be checked by a cheerful voice calling her name.

"Liz! Liz Wayburn! Hey! Wait for me. What's all the hurry?"

Only one person had ever called her Liz. She swung around in delighted greeting to a childhood friend and ally, the Vicar's young nephew. It was more than a year since they had met and he could only just have arrived or Nanty would certainly have told her of his coming. He vaulted the garden gate and joined her in the lane, eyeing her up and down in quizzical fashion and declaring that he had scarce recognised her, so fine as she was grown, "until I saw those auburn locks," he added, with an assumption of deep admiration that did not for a moment deceive the lady. Their friendship had dated from the day when a sturdy urchin, sent on a visit to his reverend uncle, had been bidden to play in the orchard. Climbing a tree and spying another child in the lane, his natural reaction to the sight of that vivid head had been to call out a teasing, "Coppernob!" He had been taken aback by the speed with which the damsel had climbed the orchard wall and advanced to the attack. Hampered by some dim chivalric notion that it wasn't cricket to hit a girl, he had tried to evade the pummelling of the hard little fists until it became a case of retaliate or cry Pax. His fancy fairly caught by the child's pluck, he had chosen the latter course. Her rage had subsided as swiftly as it had been aroused and she had made amends by lending him her handkerchief to mop a cut lip and then by admitting that she had been in the wrong to hit one who couldn't in decency hit back. Her instant recognition of his motive in suing for peace had given him a good opinion of her understanding. When he discovered that she also shared his tastes to a degree hitherto unknown in his experience, that she could be trusted not to carry tales of his more nefarious deeds to the grownups and that she paid no more heed than he did himself to the sundry cuts and bruises that their exploits entailed, he gave it as his considered opinion that she was "a regular right 'un, game as a pebble," and over the years of his intermittent visits had seen no cause to change his verdict.

Greetings exchanged and his unexpected appearance explained—he had been forbidden to go home for the vacation lest he catch some nursery complaint that was currently afflicting his brother and sisters—he was happy to stroll up the lane with Lissa and wait while she sought out shy primroses beneath the tangle of last year's dead grasses, eagerly recounting the while the various pranks with which he had relieved the tedium of study, and even suggesting helpfully that she should take off her bonnet to put the primroses in, since she had no basket with her. The advice seemed good to Lissa who still preferred to go bareheaded when she could escape authority's eye, and the collection in the discarded bonnet grew steadily, augmented by a few early violets and some wind flowers.

Presently she judged that she had sufficient and straightened up, the bonnet slung over her arm by its ribbons, the little breeze ruffling her glowing locks, already disordered by sundry treacherous twigs and brambles, as she arranged the flowers in a tight little posy and bound the stems with a wisp of grass. "Hold that for me, Ned, while I put my hat on," she demanded, handing the posy to him. He took it from her and sketched a bow, making pretence of clasping the flowers to his heart and rolling his eyes in a soulful fashion which made her giggle.

His antics evoked quite a different response from Lord Stapleford who had just tooled his curricle round the bend in the lane. Setting aside its impropriety, the sight of a handsome young man paying ardent court to a lady who, far from repulsing his advances, was laughing up into his face in a most friendly and confiding fashion, inflicted a severe shock. The introduction and explanation that followed as soon as Lissa became aware of his presence did little to soothe his unease. He found young Mr. Hetherston, with his

athletic build and open engaging manner, too
dangerously attractive to be an acceptable friend
for Lissa. If his dress indicated a leaning towards
the dandy set it was still in excellent taste and just
the style of thing to appeal to a very young lady,
thought his lordship jealously, noting the excellent relationship that flourished between the two.
When Lissa, oddly self-conscious of late if she
chanced to find herself alone with him, hesitated
over accepting a seat in the curricle, he ascribed
her reluctance to quite the wrong motives and
found difficulty in listening courteously to the
young man's enthusiastic appraisal of the splendid pair of chestnuts that he had in hand. Damn
the fellow, was his inner comment, why the devil
did he have to turn up just now? As if the position
was not already tricky enough. He favoured Mr.
Hetherston with quite a curt nod, said that no
doubt they would meet again if he was making a
prolonged stay in the neighbourhood and set the
chestnuts in motion abruptly, leaving his new
acquaintance with the notion that the much
vaunted Lord Stapleford, whom his aunt and uncle
had praised so high, was a proud sort of fellow who
obviously considered a mere stripling as being
quite beneath his touch. He made his way back to
the parsonage rather disconsolately, his pleasure
in his holiday sadly dashed.

The pair in the curricle were also unusually
silent as the short distance to the Place was swiftly
covered, Lissa submerged in the paralysing dumb-
ness that afflicted her at times since that farewell
conversation with Miss Parminter, his lordship

unsure of his ground and meditating the best way
of tackling an uncommonly nasty task. Of the two,
Lissa was the happier, content to feast her eyes on
the lean powerful fingers that controlled the
horses so easily, to glimpse, between shielding
lashes, the firm hawk-like profile, set today in lines
of unaccustomed severity. Fleetingly she wondered what had occurred to make him look so stern
and would have been horrified had she guessed
that his thoughts were concerned with her insignificant self.

A watchful groom being on the alert to take the
chestnuts, his lordship sprang down and held out a
hand to help Lissa alight. He did not at once
release her, looking down at her gravely as he said,
"There is something I wish to discuss with you.
Will you join me in the library in, let us say, half an
hour?"

Lissa, startled and a little dismayed by this
unwontedly serious manner, agreed to this and
ran off to give Madame her primroses and then to
study her appearance in the mirror as she tidied
her hair and set herself to rights before descending
to the library with a calm demeanour and an
unruly heart.

His lordship's attention to the toilet of the
chestnuts was quite shockingly perfunctory. So
preoccupied was he with the problem before him
that he would scarcely have noticed if Gellibrand
had *washed* the mud from their legs. His situation
was certainly awkward. To be warning a girl
against dalliance with an eligible young man was
in no case a congenial task. When he was in love

with the girl himself it held a dog-in-the-manger savour that was downright distasteful. Yet warned she must be. He shuddered to think of the scandal if that little scene in the lane had been witnessed by one of the neighbourhood's tabbies— or, indeed, by any matron of good repute. For a moment he toyed with the thought of getting Madame to undertake the task, but swiftly shrugged temptation aside. He was already too much obliged to the lady, and, truth to tell, he shrank from disclosing Lissa's indiscretion even to Madame.

When Lissa came quietly into the room he had still not found words in which to couch his warning so that it was the girl who broke the awkward little silence, saying shyly, "You wished to see me, my lord?"

He looked down at her, feeling the customary lift of his heart just because she was close to him and her gaze was lifted to meet his with confident trust. Then his lips twisted into a rueful grimace. "Yes. Tell me, Lissa, has Miss Parminter never spoken to you of the need for a chaperone when you wish to walk abroad?"

The tone was gentle, carrying no hint of reproof, but Lissa blushed scarlet, as though she had indeed been guilty of some impropriety, and it was a very penitent voice that replied, "Yes, my lord. She has. But I did not think—it was only as far as the village to see Nanty."

He shook his head at her. "I'm sorry, child. It seems a pity to curb your freedom. But there are always plenty of people ready to cry scandal at the first opportunity. On their lips, your innocent encounter with your childhood friend would be described as a clandestine assignation. It is very easy indeed for a young lady to suffer the stigma of being described as 'rather fast' or 'not quite the thing.' And believe me, any such hint is enough to ruin your chances of being received by the ton."

Lissa looked more puzzled than distressed. "Indeed, my lord, I am sorry for the fault and I will do my best to remember in future. But I cannot see that it matters so much in my case. Surely a governess or companion is not so carefully hedged about as is a young lady of rank? The arbiters of society are scarcely likely to concern themselves with my small misdemeanors."

This was true of course, but his lordship would have none of it. "You are too young and too attractive to walk alone," he said firmly. "You might be subjected to some indignity from strangers who did not understand your position, and since you have no parents to guide you in these matters you must submit to my wishes."

At the intimation that his lordship thought her attractive, Lissa rather lost the thread of his further remarks. In any case she found the thought of submitting to his will oddly pleasing and only wished that he would command her to some real sacrifice in his behalf. But he was already off on another track.

"It occurs to me, while on this head, that you must be turned seventeen. Did you not tell me once that you keep your birthday in May—the month in which you were brought to Stapleford? We must bestir ourselves to celebrate the day as befits so important an occasion." Seventeen was marriageable, he was thinking, but his darling was such an innocent. Why, a society damsel of two years younger would be more awake to the time of day than was his precious waif. No thought of marriage clouded the wide gaze, but, at his words, a look of deep trouble was born, so that he said urgently, "What is it? What have I said to distress you?"

She summoned a stiff little smile. "Nothing, my lord. You have only reminded me that I cannot stay here for ever. And I have been so happy here that the thought of leaving is painful. I wish that I need not grow up so quickly. I don't *want* to be seventeen," and she smiled at him, inviting him to laugh at her foolishness. But the smile was a mistake. Her self-command was not quite adequate to its maintenance and the soft lips quivered pathetically.

In the urgent desire to bring comfort to her distress his lordship forgot alike the many difficulties that beset his path and his intention to woo his love with delicate restraint. He caught her hands in his. "What nonsense is this?" he demanded brusquely. "Let me hear no more of it. This is your home. You belong here as much as I do myself."

He would have drawn her close and poured out the tale of his love and his need, but in that critical instant there came an excited knocking at the door and close upon the knock it was flung open to admit his sister, quite breathless with the haste that she had made upon her startling errand.

"Jervase! It's Grandpapa! I was looking out for your return and I have just seen him come down from the chaise. And a great heap of luggage, so it looks as if he means to stay. You were not expecting him, were you?"

Her brother loosed his grip on Lissa's hands. "No, indeed," he said thoughtfully. "Nor is it in character for him to come down on us unaware in this fashion. He is used to herald his visits with ample warning so that due care may be taken for his reception. Now what can have stirred him to such unusual activity?"

He set his hands on Mary's shoulders, spun her round and pushed her gently in the direction of the schoolroom quarters. "One thing is sure. He will expect to be received with all proper ceremony, however unexpected his coming. Hunt out your prettiest gowns, girls, and warn Madame. I'll have Mrs. Graham put dinner back an hour, so you'll have ample time for your prinking and Jacques will have time to contrive one or two side dishes worthy of our guest's attention."

And *I*, he thought soberly, may have the chance to pick up a hint as to what rumour has brought him down upon us in such a fashion, and went off to greet the Marquis.

Chapter 10

THE MARQUIS OF WRELF'S sudden arrival had indeed been prompted by a queer tale that had reached his ears. He had been spending a convivial evening at his club, beguiling the time pleasantly enough with three of his friends over the whist table and hearing all the news of the Town between the rubbers. He was finding life a trifle dull at present and wished that his grandson would make haste to tear himself away from his rustic preoccupations. That the boy should take an interest in the management of the estate was an excellent thing, though no more than was to be expected, brought up as he had been, the Marquis preened himself. But he was beginning to feel that even virtue could be carried too far. To be sure it was yet early in the Season, but he had been expecting to hear word of the young rascal's intention to return to Town ever since they left Wrelf. He had made it perfectly plain that the sinner's exile was now over and that he might consider himself forgiven. Truth to tell, London, without the boy's ridiculous starts to add savour and amusement to the social round, was something of a bore. He fell briefly into a reverie, recalling the occasions when Jervase had made his scalp prickle with apprehension—or his ribs ache with laughter. There had been the time when the lad had decked out his coat with gay knots of ribbon on breast and sleeves and challenged his friends to win themselves a guerdon at sword point while he himself defended his trophies with a buttoned foil. A dangerous play that one, and might easily have ended in a blood letting despite its friendly nature. But Jervase had a cool head on his shoulders, a good eye and a strong wrist. He had emerged unscathed with his colours intact. Only then had his interested grandsire discovered that the ribbons were tiny French tricolours, the acknowledged badge of Millicent Girling's admirers, and had promptly fallen into a rage so profound that his friends had feared an apoplexy. That memory quite spoilt his pleasure in the boy's dexterity. He shook his head to dismiss it and remembered with a grin the prank that had followed. Jervase had been visiting an old school friend who lived near Folkestone. The precious pair had purloined a couple of army mules and, attired in bonnets and hooped skirts, had raced them, side-saddle, across the Leas, to the consternation of respectable citizens who were strolling peacefully in the Sabbath calm.

His opponent's portentous cough recalled his attention to the cards. He scowled. Dilatory old fool! If he were not so damned slow in his discards one's attention would not have time to stray.

The quartet broke up at the end of the rubber, Dernstone pleading another engagement and bearing his cousin off with him. The other two sat peaceably drinking their wine until suddenly Colonel Hammond said, "I hear that youngster of yours is by way of getting legshackled at last. When's it to be announced?"

The Marquis's brows twitched to attention but there was no hint in the careless voice of the shock that he had just received. So he had been right to be suspicious of Stapleford's tarrying.

"Whence had you this?" he riposted smoothly enough.

"Oh! I ran across old Wetherley at Boodle's one day last week. Smug as bedamned over his girl's prospects. Phyllis, is it? No. Phoebe. Seems the second Sternport boy has asked permission to pay his addresses. Shouldn't think much of the match myself—bad blood on the distaff side—but Wetherley was quite set up with it. It was he who was telling me about young Jervase. Says he's the talk of the neighbourhood. Not like you to run sly, Wrelf, though I rather gathered there was something in the wind at Christmas. So he fancied the red-head after all?"

The Marquis had some difficulty in fobbing off his friend's persistence while at the same time eliciting such further information as he could gather. He was thankful when the superior attractions of whist finally persuaded Hammond to make up another table. What the devil was Stapleford about this time? He was much of a mind

to go down and see for himself. A morning call on
Mrs. Wetherley, now established in Hill Street,
only served to increase his anxieties. Even her
elation over Phoebe's success and her preoccupa-
tion with plans for an elaborate dinner party to be
given in honour of the betrothed pair did not
prevent her from launching herself on a regular
Jeremiad about Stapleford. It seemed doubtful
which she condemned the more—his earlier close
seclusion or his later absorption in the unknown
Miss Wayburn, but it soon became abundantly
clear that there was some mystery about this
young lady which his hostess was doing her best to
sniff out. Since he knew nothing, her efforts were
vain. The Viscount might have smiled to see how
the close-lipped reticence with which her hints
were rebuffed only served to convince the lady that
there was good foundation for the story. She was
pleased to believe that her own percipience had
detected Miss Wayburn's unusual quality and
quite thankful that she had never openly snubbed
the girl. She ventured a conciliatory remark on
Lady Mary's good fortune in securing so delightful
a companion to share her days, but the Marquis
brushed this aside, being in haste, he explained, to
take his leave. He was bound for Stapleford
himself, he informed her, and had only called to
enquire if she had any errands with which she
would like to charge him—a subterfuge which did
nothing to diminish the lady's indignation when
she realised that his call had lasted a scant ten
minutes. The Marquis, hard put to it to dissemble

his mingled wrath and anxiety, wasted no regrets on his social misdemeanours.

Fortunately his temper had time to cool before he reached Stapleford and he decided that there was nothing to be gained by hurling the full force of his wrath against his grandson before he had ascertained the facts. The warmth of the welcome he received still further soothed his irascibility. The boy looked amazingly well and seemed genuinely delighted to see him. Rumour was ever a lying jade. He would wait and see.

But any doubts he might have entertained about the state of his grandson's feelings were settled by one glance at the boy's face when the Comtesse de Valmeuse brought the two girls down to the drawing-room before dinner. The Viscount's orders to "put on your prettiest frocks" had been faithfully obeyed and the two presented a charming picture, Mary in crisp white muslin with a rose coloured sash and a matching fillet in her hair, Lissa in the green polonaise. But while Mary looked immature and schoolgirlish, some mischievous quirk of fate had prompted the Comtesse to dress Lissa's red-gold mane in a new fashion. Twisted into a cunning knot on top of her head it gave her added height and poise, while the glowing ringlets that fell from the knot to frame her face and throat accentuated the purity of her skin. Excitement and apprehension had brought a delicate flush to her cheeks and her eyes were huge and dark beneath the slender arched brows that had so aroused Bertha William's jealousy. Even the case-hardened Marquis caught his breath at the impact of that radiant vital charm, while Jervase momentarily forgot everything but the adoration that was writ plain on his face for all the world to read.

But Lissa, for once, was not looking at him. Her eyes had sought the Marquis, the fierce unpredictable tyrant of her imagining, whose visit seemed to presage some hidden threat to her present happiness.

That one penetrating glance had told the Marquis all that he wished to know—and a good deal that he did *not*—but the habit of a lifetime enabled him to remain outwardly imperturbable as he bowed, very much in the grand manner over the Comtesse's hand, murmuring a graceful phrase or two in appreciation of her kindness to his grand-daughter. Mary herself received a not unkindly pinch on the cheek that she had offered for his kiss and a pleasant comment on her improved appearance. Lissa was greeted courteously, the intent dark eyes so like Jervase's measuring her youth and inexperience, the keen mind already at work devising the best method of dealing with a potentially explosive situation.

By the time that dinner was done he had reached certain definite conclusions. Young as she was, the girl was already a force to be reckoned with. Apart from her innocent allure she was intelligent and quick witted, while her devotion to Stapleford Place and its historic past—and here he credited her with complete sincerity—made a strong appeal to his own sympathies, as, no doubt,

it had done to Jervase's. Moreover, despite the
cynicism born of long and intimate acquaintance
with the frail sex, he judged that the affair, though
clandestine, was wholly honourable. Setting aside
the fact that Jervase would never have permitted
his light o' love to enter his sister's orbit, the boy
was oddly strait-laced. Far more likely that his
besotted fancy would incline him towards marriage. And, to be fair, one must admire his
judgement. If the girl's breeding was all right—
and she bore every appearance of good blood—
what matter if her fortune was negligible? If the
boy's heart was really set on the chit, Wrelf could
well stand the nonsense. So why, in heaven's
name, had he withheld his confidence?

There could be only one answer. He had known
that his grandfather would refuse his consent.
While the Marquis listened with every appearance
of grave attention to the Comtesse's disquisition
on the proper preservation of family portraits, he
strove to recall just what the boy *had* told him. A
naval family, of limited means. Nothing *there* to
be ashamed of. But the name, Wayburn, failed to
strike any note of recognition—indeed it had a
plaguey commonplace ring to it. And Jessamyn
Wetherley had certainly been hinting at a scandal
of some kind. Well—he would hold his hand for the
present. It was no part of his plan to provoke a
direct confrontation with the boy. He could be
cursed obstinate when once his mind was set.
Diplomacy rather than brute force would be the
most effective weapon. But come what might, even
if he were driven to using the threat of disinheri-

tance which must be his last resource, no breath of scandal should be permitted to sully the fair name of Wrelf.

Chapter 11

THE MARQUIS pleaded the stress of his journeying as sufficient excuse for retiring early. Jervase raised an incredulous eyebrow. His grandfather might be nearing man's allotted span but never before, even after the most gruelling day in the hunting field, had he been known to admit to so shameful a weakness as fatigue. However he held his peace and dutifully escorted the old man to the state bedchamber which had been hurriedly prepared for his reception.

The unnatural calm still brooded over Stapleford Place next day. The girls were safely secluded in the schoolroom wing with Madame, and the Marquis, having commanded his grandson's attendance, spent the forenoon in visiting some of the farms that comprised the estate and, in general, commending the novice's efforts at good stewardship. He then announced his intention of looking up one or two old cronies who had not betaken themselves to Town. From this expedition, which had included a call on the unsuspect-

ing Mr. Hetherston, he returned with a grim set to
his mouth and a cold fury in his eye that plainly
warned of storms to come.

Yet still he held his hand. He had intimated that
he did not desire the presence of the girls at dinner
so that only the three of them sat down to the meal.
The Comtesse seemed unusually withdrawn. In
marked contrast to the pleasant informality of the
previous evening, conversation was on a very
stilted plane. Jervase could not but admire the
practised ease with which his elders maintained a
gentle flow of meaningless vapidities when their
minds were quite obviously preoccupied with other
interests. There was no need for him to make more
than a token contribution; which was just as well.
He had a notion that he would need all his mental
energies in the impending conflict with his
grandsire. For there could be no more putting off. If
the Marquis did not broach the subject of Lissa
Wayburn, then he himself must do so. And he
would be thankful to be done with pretence. He was
still deeply ashamed of the way in which he had
misled his grandfather about Lissa's history and it
was no excuse that at that time he had not realised
how much she had come to mean to him. Now that
his mind was irrevocably set on marriage he owed
his grandfather the whole truth at the earliest
possible moment.

It was disconcerting, though, when the Comtesse had made her excuses, to find himself quite
unable to assess the Marquis's attitude. There had
been stern reproof in the brief sentences that had
invited explanation of the deception that he had

practised. But when the fault had been admitted
and due contrition expressed, the older man had
listened quietly enough to the long and complicated story which was laid before him. Halting
and diffident at first, its delivery had gained pace
and confidence until it reached the point at which
the Marquis's own unexpected arrival had barely
prevented a declaration of love.

Quietly he had listened, which was sadly out of
character. Only once had he shown any visible
emotion, and that was to smooth away an
irrepressible grin at the hints of mythical grandeur which had so set Mrs. Wetherley by the ears.
That certainly tickled his wry sense of humour.
But beneath this lighter mood a sense of deep
alarm was growing within him. He had been
considerably disturbed when he heard Hetherston's account of the boy's dealings with his waif.
Now, listening to the tale from his own lips, this
anxiety increased. This was no sickly greenhead's
fancy as in the case of Millicent Girling. The
protective tenderness, the quiet statement of his
intentions, even the absence of fulsome praise of
his darling, were all of a man. In the silence that
ensued when his grandson had made an end the
Marquis suddenly, unwilling, recalled a fleeting
memory some fifty years old. His own first love
had been given to a girl scarcely more suitable
than the boy's Lissa. There had never been any
question of marriage, for his bride had already
been selected for him by his parents, the betrothal
announced. The girl he had so foolishly loved had
been hastily whisked away out of his ken and

married off to a country squire of comfortable means. He never knew just how it had been managed but he always suspected that his father had provided a dowry that had made the girl's charms quite irresistible. He had lost track of her after her marriage—and his own marriage had been quite satisfactory. His wife had been perfectly docile and having supplied him with an heir had been complaisant enough when he chose to follow his roving fancy wherever it led. Not that he had been a great rake; too fastidious for that, with little liking for bought caresses. But naturally over the years there had been a number of pleasant little affairs. He felt that he had arrived at a very just appreciation of the proper place for women in a man's life. So why, at this damnably inconvenient moment, should he suddenly recall a rapture once briefly glimpsed, and feel an uncomfortable degree of pity for the grandson who must suffer a like disappointment?

His voice was gruff with sympathy as he said slowly, "It won't do, lad. You must know yourself it won't do."

No answer. Only the boy's lips folded together in a stern line and the dark head lifted a trifle.

Carefully he went on, "Even if we could make your absurd tale of royal blood stick—and you must know the impossibility of that—it would make no difference. I say nothing against the girl. To all appearances she's a thoroughbred. But appearances aren't everything. Nor would I cavil at her lack of fortune." He noted thankfully that Jervase was listening attentively, his pose a little relaxed. This was the right tack, the safe tack. "But there's more to it than that. I said just now that appearances aren't everything. Sooner or later breeding always tells. Some day you will be Wrelf. Do you want to run the risk that your son will be a moonling like Sternport? Or maybe a cripple or some perverted maniac?"

His sympathetic attitude had served him well. It had inhibited open defiance and gained him time for manoeuvre. To have provoked the boy to desperate action at this stage would have been fatal. He went on, slowly, thoughtfully, "Someone, somewhere, knows the girl's story. If we can discover the truth—if you can prove to me that she is fit to mate with you, then I will not refuse my consent. Otherwise—" He shrugged. "You are of age. You will go the way of your choosing. But it will be a sorry business."

The quiet words were more forceful than a blow. They foreshadowed the loss of his birthright. And while a man could always make his way, while, indeed, he would still have a comfortable competence to call his own, yet for Lissa he wanted everything that rank and wealth could offer. Eagerly he snatched at the tenuous hope of a happy solution.

"Her foster mother knows nothing. As I grew to know Lissa, so my curiosity grew to know her story, but the woman had nothing to tell except the name of the lawyer who brought the child to her. Whitehead. He *must* know something and may be persuaded to reveal it. That's the obvious starting point, isn't it, Sir?"

It was the Marquis's turn to feel all the
discomfort of a guilt that stemmed from treachery
to one who loved and trusted him. It must be in the
highest degree improbable that the girl's birth
should be stainless. But by sending his grandson
off on what could only be a fool's errand he would
gain a further breathing space. Time—that precious commodity—to attack from another angle.
The memory of his own youthful folly had given
him the notion of tackling the girl. If he could get
rid of her while Jervase was away—buy her off,
perhaps? There might even be some willing suitor
who would take her off his hands if she were well
enough dowered. She was enough to stir any man's
blood, and with money as well—

He opened his campaign early the next day, as
soon as Jervase had taken his leave, asking if the
girls might be excused their studies for once, so
that they could ride with him. He wished, he said,
to see what progress his grand-daughter had made
in the equestrian art under her brother's tuition.
The Comtese eyed him thoughtfully as she gave
pleasant assent to the suggestion. The girls went
off to change, Lissa, who loved the horses and rode
whenever opportunity offered, in high glee. Mary
shivering with apprehension.

Nevertheless she acquitted herself well enough
to earn a word of commendation. At Lissa he shook
his head. "Neck or nothing, that's you, Miss,
plenty of pluck but little sense, and no way for a
young lady to ride," and was startled when she
only grinned in friendly fashion, obviously caring
nothing for his opinion one way or the other.

Reluctantly he admitted to himself that he was uncommonly taken with the chit. For one with so little experience she showed up damned well on a horse—light hands and a natural easy seat. On good terms with the beast she rode, too, and he not the easiest of mounts, a nappy young chestnut. Well matched, the pair of them, he conceded. What was more the girl seemed quite unmindful of her own attractions—made no attempt to play off her sex—behaved more like a lively schoolboy than a young woman.

None of this, of course, made any difference to his determination to be rid of her as soon as possible. Indeed, the better he liked her the more dangerous did she seem. There was no time to be lost. He dismissed Mary to the schoolroom but put a detaining hand on Lissa's wrist, saying that he would be glad of the favour of a short talk with her. It was high time, he felt, that they improved their acquaintance.

There could be no question of refusing what was tantamount to a royal command. Quaking inwardly but with her head well up, Lissa preceded him into the library and accepted the chair that he indicated. My lord did not choose to be seated but prowled restlessly across to the windows, finding some awkwardness in initiating a difficult subject. But he had never been one to shirk his fences, though he felt a slight qualm as he turned towards the girl. She looked so small and defenceless, quite lost in the massive chair, and he seemed to tower over her. Involuntarily his voice softened a little as he said gravely, "There are one or two questions I would like to ask you, Miss Wayburn. I trust you will pardon any seeming presumption in one who is not only old enough to be your grandfather but who is also sincerely concerned for your welfare."

Lissa's voice failed her at this ominous preamble. She stammered out something that might be taken for assent and essayed a smile. The Marquis hardened his heart and pressed on. Little by little he drew from her all the details of her story and as her tension relaxed under his matter-of-fact questioning she spoke quite simply and naturally of her plans for the future and of how Lord Stapleford had promised to use his interest to help her to a situation when she was ready.

Throughout this frank recital the Marquis continued his restless prowling. She came to an end with a tiny shrug of resignation and raised her eyes to his, clearly inviting his judgement. He sighed deeply. It was a genuine sigh, for he was truly sorry for the little creature trapped in a web that was none of her weaving. And at the sound of the sigh and the sight of his sombre expression the faint gleam of hope left the appealing young face and her pretty colour faded. She made neither protest nor plea. Only her hands clenched together in her lap as she waited dumbly.

"Don't look so anxious, my dear," said the Marquis gently. "We will see to it that something is arranged for you so that you may be comfortable even though your present plans must be changed. For I have to tell you that it really will not do for you to remain here. It was the rumour of your presence which brought me down from Town to see for myself, for I could not credit the scandal that is circulating about your relations with Lord Stapleford. Now, no need to get on your high ropes, child—" for she had risen and was fronting him with a steady dignity that belied her youth—"I can see for myself that it is all perfectly innocent, and all the fault of that caper-witted grandson of mine. I gave him a rare trimming, I can tell you, for he is quite old enough to have taken more thought for how the matter would appear to the outside world. The thing is, I am sure you would not wish to harm his prospects despite his foolish behaviour, so kind as you say he has been to you. And *that*, my dear, so long as you remain under his roof, is just what you stand in danger of doing."

The girl's control in face of this rebuke was quite creditable. She coloured up finely but her voice was low and steady as she said, "You are very right, my lord Marquis. I am indeed deeply indebted to Lord Stapleford and would do whatever I might to serve him. Pray tell me how best I may do so."

Once again the Marquis's conscience gave him an uncomfortable moment. The little thing was so confiding, so innocent. He reminded himself that he had spoken truth when he had said that he was concerned for her welfare. For what would become of her if Stapleford, denied marriage, should choose to make her his mistress? No doubt they would be blissfully happy for a while and in Stapleford's case little harm would be done. But for the girl it would be the first step in a descending spiral that could end in disease and direst poverty on London's streets. He could do better for her than that.

"The trouble is, my dear, that you are too pretty by far," he began, and smiled to see her startled expression. No one had ever called her pretty before. "Add to that the fact that you have been seen everywhere with my grandson and that he has lingered at Stapleford instead of returning to Town for the Season, and you will see that there was ample ground for gossip. I regret that I must speak in such plain terms to one so young, but it would do Stapleford a great deal of harm to have it said that he had seduced a mere child, his sister's companion, and living under his own roof. Though it is not generally known I am in hopes that he will shortly be forming a very eligible alliance with a young lady whose parents would take grave exception to such libertine behaviour."

Good God! The girl was going to faint! At the Marquis's optimistic, not to say mendacious, account of his grandson's intentions, every vestige of colour had fled and she put out one hand blindly as though to ward off some threatened danger. Hurriedly the Marquis pressed her back into the chair and sought about him for some restorative. There was only the brandy that stood on a small Pembroke table near the hearth and he was a little doubtful of the effect of so powerful a stimulant. Nevertheless he hastily splashed some into a goblet and held it to the girl's lips. She tried to turn her head aside but his lordship insisted, tilting the glass so that she was forced to swallow some of the horrid stuff. She shuddered at the fierce bite of it but it certainly dispelled the faintness that had for a moment threatened to overwhelm her. Presently she was able to sit up and murmur her thanks for his lordship's attentions. He eyed her uneasily, feeling that it might be wiser to defer the rest of his remarks until she was more completely recovered, but the girl herself took the initiative.

"What do you wish me to do, my lord? You said that I could be helpful if I would. Shall I return to my foster mother?"

It was gallantly said, with no hint of how dismal such a prospect now appeared. But the suggestion did not appeal to the Marquis at all.

"I do not think that is the best answer," he said consideringly, and did not add that *any* answer which left her within Stapleford's reach would be totally unacceptable. "It would be better to follow the original plan. But instead of waiting till next year we will set about it at once. I am quite as well placed as Stapleford in the matter of finding you a suitable post and have no doubt that in a little while we shall hit upon the very thing. But it is essential that you should leave at once, for only in that way can the scandal be scotched. So until we find you a situation I propose to place you for a time in the home of a relative of mine, a distant cousin who resides in Torquay. She is elderly and lives very retired but you will be quite safe and comfortable with her. Now don't worry your little head about anything. Just look forward to a delightful holiday beside the sea. I believe sea bathing is all the crack nowadays—you will enjoy that, won't you? I will arrange that you are amply supplied with funds. There are some very good shops in Torquay. You will like to choose some pretty fripperies after living so quietly here. I shall write to my cousin at once to advise her of your coming and my own coachman shall drive you down, with one of the maids for propriety's sake." And he sighed with relief and some complaisance at having handled a delicate task with both good sense and due sympathy, and proceeded to indite his letter to his cousin, engaging her good offices for the unfortunate young girl whom he would shortly be consigning to her care.

Chapter 12

THE MARQUIS might have spared his pains. In his dealings with Lissa he had made two grave errors. He had forgotten that she had not been reared in the tradition of unquestioning obedience that was so carefully inculcated in the well-bred society maidens to whom he was accustomed. Lissa had learned to fight her own battles, make her own decisions. Even so, dazed and stricken as she was by the news of Jervase's impending betrothal, she might well have submitted to his lordship's kindly management with the expected docility if he had not made the further mistake of treating her as though she was a child to be cozened with promises of treats in store, and, above all, if he had not offered her money.

That final insult did more than the brandy to revive her failing spirit, and set her, when she had reached the seclusion of her own room, to thinking more carefully about the whole scheme. Why should she be hurried away to distant Torquay as though she had committed some crime and had to

be hidden? It was reasonable to suppose, as the
Marquis had explained, that Mary would be
distressed at her going, and she had quite readily
agreed not to mention her approaching departure
to anyone until he had first completed his
arrangements to send his grand-daughter to
London. She should go on a long visit to her Aunt
Goldsborough and by the time that she came home
would have grown accustomed to doing without
Lissa. But when it came to directing *her* comings
and goings, it did not take Lissa long to decide that
the Marquis had not the shadow of a right to
dictate to her. If her going from the Place was
necessary for Jervase's happiness, then certainly
she would go. But she would go in her own time and
to a destination of her own choosing.

For the moment she must put her own plans
aside. Mary was delighted with the prospect of a
visit to London though regretful that Lissa was
not to share the treat. There was an excited bustle
of preparation and packing. The Comtesse, who
had business affairs of her own to attend to in
Town, had agreed to act as escort for the journey,
though she would be returning almost immediately. She suggested that Lissa might like to go
home to Nanty for a brief visit, but when the girl
returned a noncommittal answer she did not press
the matter.

In the intervals of helping to choose the dresses
that Mary should take and listening to the
promises of frequent letters to be written and gifts
to be brought back, Lissa wrestled with her own
problem. She was not quite penniless. There were a

few guineas that Nanty had saved for her from her
wages at Bank Sykes, and since coming to live at
the Place she had received a regular allowance of
pin money along with Mary. But that would not
last long. She must find work quickly—and how
was that to be done without references or friends to
speak for her?

Comfort, and the germ of a plan, came to her in
the guise of a letter from Miss Parminter which
was delivered on the very day that the Comtesse
and Mary left for London. At least she had one
staunch friend she thought, carrying the epistle
out into the Italian garden to read at leisure.
Perhaps Miss Parminter would help her to find
work, though she was doubtful as to whether the
funds at her disposal were sufficient to pay her fare
on the London stage. But when she had broken the
wafer and unfolded the single sheet, *that* problem
at least was resolved. For the letter, penned in
haste, advised her that Miss Parminter was about
to leave London. General Carnforth had been
persuaded to remove to Bath, in the hope that a
course of the waters would benefit his health. She
was to accompany him on the journey and see him
settled into his lodging, but after that her plans
were uncertain. However, since Bath was only
forty miles distant from Stapleford, it might be
possible for Lissa to pay her a short visit, since she
intended to take a holiday, after the exacting task
of nursing the old man, before resuming her duties
at Stapleford Place.

Here was much food for thought. Lissa walked
slowly back to the house turning over in her mind

how best she could make use of the new state of
affairs. Miss Parminter would receive her at once,
she was sure, however inconvenient, and Bath
would be a very good place in which to seek
employment. There were a great many girls'
schools in the city and with Miss Parminter to
speak for her she might possibly obtain a post as
an under-governess in one of them. Absently she
tidied away a few last minute trifles that Mary had
left lying about and began to bundle together a pile
of out-grown garments that the Comtesse had
asked her to send down to the Vicarage for
distribution to needy families. Her fingers worked
slowly for her mind was busily forming and
rejecting plans by which she might slip away from
the village and travel to Bath unobserved. It must
be soon, or, knowing the Marquis, she was like to
find herself carried to Torquay willy-nilly. Any
day now would see the return of his messenger and
after that her departure would not be long delayed.
She could almost hear the old autocrat declaring
impatiently that there was no need to waste time in
packing. She could buy all that she would need in
those admirable shops in Torquay. Packing! Her
hands abandoned their desultory activities as she
conceived a notion of such delightful simplicity
that, test it as she would, she did not see how it
could fail. It would mean enlisting Ned Hetherston's aid, but there could be no difficulty about
that. She had too often helped him out of awkward
fixes in the past to stand in any doubt of his
willingness to serve her. A glance at the schoolroom clock informed her that the hour was not yet

eleven. There would be time to seek out Ned before
her early nuncheon. If only he had not elected to go
off on a long ramble, as he was still prone to do!

But fortune smiled on her enterprise. She did not
even need to call at the Vicarage, for she
encountered Ned hacking gently down the very
lane that had been the scene of their last meeting.
His manner was a little stiff at first, so that, had
her mind not been so preoccupied by her urgent
need, she would have been asking what she had
done to merit his displeasure. But as soon as young
Mr. Hetherston heard her story—for she told him
only of her earnest wish to leave the Place and
journey secretly to join Miss Parminter in Bath—
he unbent swiftly enough. Still resenting the
cavalier treatment he had received at Lord Stapleford's hands, he was only too ready to put his own
interpretation on Lissa's story. If Stapleford had
been pestering her with unwanted attentions that
would be reason enough for her wish to escape.
And since her destination was a highly respectable lodging in Gay Street where she proposed to
put herself under the protection of the formidable
Miss Parminter, there could be no possible harm in
helping her. In fact he would be delighted to throw
a rub in his lordship's path. He *did* wonder
whether he ought not to suggest that she seek
shelter with his aunt, but on second thoughts
realised that this would place his uncle in a rather
difficult position vis-a-vis his patron. He then
joined wholeheartedly in devising a plan that
should be absolutely foolproof.

"Could you be ready to leave tomorrow?" he

asked, after much animated discussion. "The thing is, you see, I had already told my aunt that I was thinking of visiting friends in Warminster for a day or two, and my uncle said I might take the gig. So if you could be ready and we arranged to meet somewhere, I could see you safely to your destination myself and no one would think anything of my absence. Could you manage to pack your gear and smuggle it out of the house without any of the servants noticing? For if you're spotted and we chance to be seen together, it'll be all over the village that we've eloped before the cat can lick her ear."

"That's just it," explained Lissa with an echo of her former gaiety. "It was the packing that made me think of you."

He grinned. "Your flattery overwhelms me, ma'am. No use for my manifest virtues as an escort—my strong right arm, my vast worldly knowledge, not to mention my entertaining conversation. No! You think of packing—as wearisome a task as the mind of man can conceive—and think at once of me. My thanks!"

"No, but do but listen, Ned," she urged, with no more than a polite smile for his raillery. "I was packing up some of Mary's dresses to give to your uncle for some of his poor families when I saw at once that nothing could be simpler than to pack a few necessities for myself and bring them down to the Vicarage at the same time. You could conceal them in the gig, under a rug or something, couldn't you?"

Her ally admitted that such a task ought not to

be beyond his powers of ingenuity and they arranged to meet at the point where the Stapleford lane joined the main Warminster road at ten o'clock next day. Lissa would need to start betimes since she would have to walk to the rendezvous, but they dared not arrange to meet any nearer the village. Nor must she linger any longer now, for fear she would be missed. Ned walked beside her a little way, leading his horse, his pleasant countenance suddenly subdued with embarrassment. "I say, Lissa," he blurted out abruptly. "Are the dibs in tune? I mean to say—well—I know you're going to stay with friends and all that, but it won't do to go without a penny in your pocket. It just so happens that I'm pretty well in funds just now, so if a trifling loan would make you feel more comfortable—" His faltering phrases died away and he studied the dusty lane beneath their feet with deep intensity. Lissa caught his free hand in hers and carried it to her face, rubbing her cheek against it like an affectionate kitten. "Bless you, Ned," she said with warm gratitude. "You're a dear. But it's all right. I have sufficient for my needs."

He was not wholly reassured but knew better than to press the matter further. Presently he had the brilliant notion of slipping a purse into the bundle that was to be entrusted to him and felt a little happier. He turned back at the Stapleford Place gates, trotting cheerfully down the lane, his mind pleasantly engaged with plans for tomorrow's expedition. It would be a jolly good lark, he decided, unaware that his fellow traveller was

thinking that she had never been so unhappy
before. She must *look* her usual self, for Ned had
noticed nothing amiss, but there was an ache in
her throat that made speaking painful and only by
a determined effort could she hold back the tears at
the thought that tomorrow she must say good-bye
to the Place, perhaps for ever.

Yet she was fully as anxious to be gone as even
the Marquis himself could have wished, and
dreaded the possibility that the Viscount might
return before she was safe away. She had always
known that he was not for her. But so long as he
was not pledged to another she had been free to
worship him, to sun herself in his manifest liking
which, of late, had seemed so warmly protective,
and to dream her shy girlish dreams of serving
him in some way that would establish her firmly in
his affection. When chance had offered she had
stored up pictures of him in her mind; the laughter
in the dark eyes over Mary's antics in the hooped
skirt; the arrogant tilt of his head for encroaching
sycophancy or hypocrisy; the gentle dexterity of
the lean brown fingers in handling a sick hound.
Now those pictures were all that she might
honourably keep. The thought of seeing him
again, of touching in greeting the fingers that
could set her pulses racing, was not to be endured.
That the parting must come she had accepted as
the price of her secret rapture. But it had come so
soon and so suddenly that she felt as though her
heart was being wrenched in two. At one moment
she wished him only happiness and contentment
in his marriage, in the next she was consumed

with a fury of hatred for his unknown bride that shocked even herself. At the very thought of the girl her fingers crooked themselves into claws, avid to scratch and strangle.

She shook her head fiercely as though to deny her desolation and quickened her pace. She had not been missed, though Janet was waiting to serve her solitary nuncheon. She had little appetite and only toyed with the breast of chicken cooked in white wine sauce which was one of her favourites. Janet was reproachful, trying to coax her to eat. Auntie, she said, had ordered this specially tempting meal knowing that Miss Lissa would be feeling lonesome all by herself, and declaring that there was nothing like good victuals for cheering a body up. And see, here were the very first of the strawberries and a pitcher of cream to pour over them. Lissa was insensibly comforted by the girl's concern and by Mrs. Graham's thought for her, but it was difficult to force even strawberries and cream past that lump in her throat and she was thankful enough to lay down the spoon when the schoolroom door opened and the Marquis walked in.

He nodded dismissal to Janet and apologised punctiliously to Lissa for interrupting her meal and for coming to see her in his riding dress. Almost as though she was grown up, she thought fleetingly, and then forgot everything else as he went on to inform her that her journey was all arranged for the following day. The groom who had carried his letter to Torquay had just returned and Miss Granger had written to say that it would be quite convenient to receive his young charge. "So you can get that wench to pack your belongings. Graham's niece, isn't she? Seems a sensible sort of girl. You'd best take her along for your abigail. There's no need to make a very early start—you'll be bound to spend one night on the road in any case. But Sansom assures me that there's very decent accommodation to be had in Crewkerne, or in Honiton if you make good speed. I've ordered the carriage for ten o'clock—that will be time enough. And as I shan't see you again before you leave, here's a little something to buy yourself a pretty gown or two, as I promised."

He took Lissa's unresisting fingers and folded them round a small package, smiling at her kindly, and somehow she managed to murmur a rather stilted thank you.

"Now cheer up," he exhorted her. "Be a good child, and I'll send you word as soon as I find a suitable opening for you."

She thanked him once more in a small colourless voice, but she was already recovering from the shock of his announcement and thanking heaven that her own plans were so well advanced. She bade him a dutiful farewell and then, quite as though it was an afterthought asked if she might have the use of the pony carriage during the afternoon to deliver the bundles—she indicated them—to the Vicarage. Lord Wrelf was vaguely uneasy. She would be bound to mention her going and he would very much rather that no one outside his personal household knew of it. He said that one of the grooms could perfectly well discharge the

simple task and no need to put herself to any
trouble over it. But when Lissa said that she would
like to say good-bye to the Hetherstons and thank
them for all their kindness to her he could scarcely
persist in his objections. He gave permission,
reminding himself that Hetherston would be
heartily of his own opinion as to the wisdom of
sending the girl away. A word in the good man's
ear, and Jervase would never learn her whereabouts from *him*.

Chapter 13

IT WAS oppressively hot. Even the leaves of the magnificent trees that clothed the slopes of Beechen Cliff hung limp, with no breath of air to set them whispering. Lissa pushed back damp tendrils of hair from an aching brow. She had already discarded her hat and wished once more that she had been able to include one or two of her thinner dresses in the bundle that Ned had smuggled into the gig. But she had been forced to limit its contents to such items as Janet would not think of packing for the journey to Torquay. The snuff brown dress which Nanty had chosen for the start of her great adventure was heavy in this weather and was not helped by the fact that she had grown so much that it was uncomfortably tight across the breast and round the arms. She thought wistfully of the purse of money that she had found when she unpacked her bundle and wondered if she might use some of it to buy herself just one muslin gown. But the prices in the shops on Milsom Street had frightened her and she did not choose to squander Ned's money on high-priced luxuries. It would have to be paid back as soon as she had found work.

Dear Ned! He had managed her escape beautifully. They had stabled Dandy and the gig in Warminster with Ned's friends and had hired a light chaise for the remainder of the journey. The friends were a young couple only recently married. They had accepted the arrival of a strange young female without question and offered cheerful hospitality in the most informal way. When Ned had spoken of escorting Miss Wayburn to Bath, Michael had insisted on lending him his own covert-hack. Lissa had been sorry to leave their friendly menage.

The house in Gay Street that General Carnforth had hired was both elegant and comfortable and despite their unheralded arrival and the fact that she herself had only been installed in it for two days, Miss Parminter's welcome had been warm and sincere, bringing comfort and reassurance to a sore heart. General Carnforth paid little heed to the unexpected addition to his household. By a blessed dispensation of Providence he had come across a former comrade in arms among the valetudinarians who gathered daily in the Pump Room. The two had served together under Cornwallis and since they spent their days very contentedly re-fighting old campaigns and criticising the conduct of the current ones, both gentlemen were agreed that the waters of Bath and the treatment they were receiving were highly beneficial. Since the General always breakfasted in his own room he and Lissa very rarely met and Miss Parminter was free to spend most of her time with her young guest. Today, however, she had gone to visit a friend who conducted a very select seminary for young ladies in fashionable Bathwick, and Lissa had been left to her own devices. It was doubtless wrong in her to venture out alone, but having studied her reflection in the sober stuff gown and with her hair hidden under an old-fashioned bonnet borrowed from her hostess she felt she could pass for an abigail going on an errand for her mistress and should be safe from molestation, Miss Parminter having most particularly warned her against the demi-beaux and rakehells who infested the city.

Miss Parminter was regretfully coming to the conclusion that the air of Bath did not suit her young friend. During the month which had passed since her arrival she had grown listless and heavy-eyed as though she had slept badly. She ate little—Lissa, who, on her first arrival at Stapleford Place had found the art of the chef so irresistible that she had actually reproved the child for greed. And all of this was a great pity for it must militate against a splendid scheme of her own for securing the girl's future.

It had long been her intention, when she had saved a sufficient sum, to go into partnership with her friend in Bathwick. She had hoped that this happy day would arrive in some two or three years' time when Lady Mary would be old enough to dispense with her services. But if she could persuade Miss Meredith that the sum she had saved was sufficient—or if, in his present un-wontedly benign mood, General Carnforth could be persuaded that a loan to a thriving educational establishment would be a sound investment, then her dream would become fact and what was more she would be in a position to offer Lissa suitable work under her own guidance. Not a word of this had she divulged to the girl herself since it was dependent on so many "ifs," though she had felt quite guilty at leaving the child to entertain herself, so low spirited as she had been since her arrival. But it was growing increasingly difficult to pacify her with assurances that the help that she gave with domestic duties and the pleasure that Miss Parminter took in her society were adequate return for the cost of her keep. While as for her refusal to buy that charming sprigged muslin gown, or to allow Miss Parminter to buy it for her—well, really! One could carry indepen-dence too far!

It had been a great pleasure to the lonely spinster to have an agreeable companion to share her explorations of the ancient city. While paying just tribute to its many modern improvements, both ladies preferred to delve into the past. Miss Parminter's knowledge of the antiquities was far superior but it was Lissa's lively imagination that peopled the place with the marching legions or the mythical court of King Bladud. Briefly, while absorbed in these flights of fancy, she would seem once more the vivid eager child who had first won Miss Parminter's regard. But such moments were rare. For the greater part of the time she was

unnaturally subdued—compliant and helpful, but
withdrawn into a world of her own. She had, of
course, told her hostess the whole story of her
sudden arrival in so far as it concerned others. Of
her own hurt and grief she made no mention and
Miss Parminter was too sensitive a woman to
probe the secrets of the child's heart. She had felt
herself bound to concur with the Marquis's point of
view and thought that under the circumstances he
had acted both wisely and kindly, though she was
well pleased that Lissa had chosen rather to come
to her. Privately she thought the girl would have
been more sensible to have accepted the money
that was offered, but this opinion she kept to
herself, respecting the principles that had dictated
the refusal. The package had been left unopened
on the library table enclosed in a brief note which
expressed Miss Wayburn's polite regret that she
could not accept either the Marquis's plans or his
money and had made her own arrangements. An
affectionate note for Nanty, begging her not to be
anxious since Lissa would be safe with friends,
had been delivered by Ned under cover of darkness, a touch of drama which had delighted that
young man. Unfortunately the message did little
to soothe the poor woman's fears, for who could the
unknown friends be?

She might have been comforted could she have
been privileged to overhear a conversation in
progress in a certain neatly furnished parlour on
the outskirts of Bathwick. Miss Meredith listened
to Edith Parminter's detailed exposition of her
young friend's dilemma with absorbed interest.

The plan of setting up a partnership must be reserved for further consideration. The sum that Edith mentioned was modest. On the other hand Bathwick was developing rapidly and she had a satisfactory waiting list of hopeful pupils. She would like to extend her accommodation for parlour boarders, but that meant building—a heavy expense. Edith's contribution would be useful there, but she would prefer to consult with her lawyer before reaching a decision.

As though to make amends for this businesslike attitude, her interest in Lissa's story was sympathetic. She would like to help. But could Edith vouch for the girl? Miss Meredith's pupils were drawn mainly from the daughters of the squirearchy, leavened by an occasional offshoot of the minor aristocracy. No governess, however junior, could be admitted to that select dovecot unless her character and references were unimpeachable.

Angry colour suffused Miss Parminter's cheeks. "She has been educated under my personal supervision and has had the inestimable advantage of being reared in the Wyncaster household. It is only the misfortune of Lord Stapleford's having begun to pay her such distinguishing attention that has cast her upon the world at so tender an age. Lord Wrelf himself was willing to sponsor her, but her delicacy of principle persuaded her rather to apply to me."

Miss Meredith's eyes brightened. "The Wrelf connection could be very useful to us," she pointed out. "A favourable word from *that* quarter—" She shrugged. "In the meantime—" her manner grew

brisk—"your protégée can make herself useful
immediately if she so chooses. Miss Beaton has
foolishly contracted the mumps from her small
brother. It is most inconvenient since I have three
girls staying on at school over the holidays. Their
parents are abroad. Major Miller is serving in
India. Miss Beaton was charged with the task of
supervising their activities. If Miss Wayburn
wishes to earn her keep she may take Miss
Beaton's place. Naturally I would not expect to pay
a salary since there is really no work involved. It is
just a matter of joining the girls on their little
excursions and seeing that they come to no harm.
She would be housed and fed and I would have the
opportunity of assessing her character and ability
for myself."

It was not to be expected that Miss Parminter
would accept much meagre terms for a task that
she well knew to be far more onerous than
teaching. The charge of three lively girls—four-
teen-year-old twins and a younger sister—imbued
with holdiay high spirits, was by no means the
sinecure that Miss Meredith had implied. She
succeeded in wringing from that lady the offer of a
small salary in addition to board and lodging and
promised to put the suggestion before Miss
Wayburn. The two ladies then exchanged dignified farewells, each with an increased respect for
the other's business acumen and no diminution of
goodwill.

Under the shelter of a low hanging branch Lissa
started awake, yawned and stretched in brief
contentment from a dream in which she had been

back at the Place. Coming fully awake, with the
now familiar sinking of her spirits as she recalled
her true situation, she wondered for the hundredth
time if Jervase had yet returned from his unexpected journey to London. Had he, perhaps, gone
there to wait upon the girl that he was to marry?
Surreptitiously she had searched the columns of
the *Morning Post* each day, expecting yet dreading
to see the announcement of his betrothal. No word
had come from Ned, the only person who knew her
direction. She was as much cut off from her former
life as though she had suddenly been transported
to another planet.

Chapter 14

JERVASE'S VISIT to London proved to be frustrating in the extreme. He made a good start. Mr. Whitehead, it transpired, was well known in his professional capacity to several of Jervase's friends who pronounced him to be both able and discreet. There was no difficulty in tracing him either to the prosperous looking chambers where he conducted his business affairs or to his private address. But there success ended and the obstacles began. Mr. Whitehead was away on business in the north and no one could say exactly when he would return. It might be as long as a sennight.

In the event it was ten days, and for that seemingly interminable time Jervase kicked his heels in maddening idleness and wondered how he had ever contrived to pass the time in former years. It was not that there was any lack of diversion. As soon as it was known that he was back in Town he was positively inundated with invitations to a dozen different parties and might take his choice between a musical soirée, a drum, and a grand ball

given by the Sternports to honour Miss Wetherley.
Or if he preferred entertainment in a lighter vein
he might join a party in Hyde Park and stake his
blunt on a race between two sturdy piglets ridden
by pet monkeys.

With shocking lack of appreciation he dropped
the rest of the elegantly superscribed missives on
to his writing table without even bothering to open
them. There was nothing from Stapleford so they
held no interest for him. Somehow, between riding
and driving out into the country with one or two
like minded friends, putting in a little practice with
the foils and an occasional rubber of picquet, he
managed to get through the days. He even had the
grace to laugh at himself for turning so soon, even
before matrimony had contributed its well-known
sobering influence, into the very epitome of the
country squire who couldn't abide Town life and
longed only to return to his ancestral acres. Of
course when he married Lissa it would be different.
It would be amusing to show her the sights and
take her to all the ton parties. He would enjoy *her*
enjoyment. But even so he rather thought that
they would spend most of their time in the country.
He yawned and went off to bed at the indecently
early hour of eleven. He must be up betimes next
day, for the elusive Mr. Whitehead had at last
returned to Town and had made an appointment to
see him at noon.

As was only to be expected he was by far too
early for this all-important engagement and was
ushered into a small ante-room where he paced
impatiently from chair to window until Mr.

Whitehead should be at liberty. Presently he saw from his window the clerk who had admitted him obsequiously assisting a heavily veiled female to enter a closed carriage. That presumably was the client who had preceded him, for almost immediately the door opened and the clerk announced that Mr. Whitehead could see him now.

The lawyer's appearance came as a surprise. Jervase had somehow assumed that he would be elderly. But the man who came forward to greet him and to apologise pleasantly for the inordinate delay in arranging the meeting could not be much more than thirty. Seeing him so taken aback Mr. Whitehead said at once, "Perhaps your lordship was expecting to see my uncle? I regret that ill health compelled his retirement last year. But I shall be happy to offer you any service that lies within my power."

There was something immediately likeable about this quiet-voiced, blunt-featured young man, so different from the gimlet-eyed, sharp spoken creation of Jervase's imagining. He found it easier than he had thought to explain his situation and his problem.

Mr. Christopher Whitehead listened attentively, making neither comment nor query until the tale was done. There followed a long thoughtful pause before he said quietly, "An interesting case, my lord. I must make it clear from the outset that I, personally, cannot be of any assistance to you. It was, of course, my uncle who originally placed the child with Mrs. Wayburn, but I very much doubt it he ever knew the truth about the child's parentage.

If he did, he is, alas! unable to impart his knowledge. He suffered a severe seizure last summer which has impaired his faculties. He can neither speak nor write. However, there is one person, a client of mine, who may be in a position to help you. The business is, of course, highly confidential. I could not furnish you with names or directions. But I *could* make representations on your behalf if you wish me to do so."

"Most certainly I do," said Jervase emphatically, "and with the utmost despatch."

The lawyer smiled slightly. "You realise that my client may refuse outright? Or that, if the information is forthcoming, it may not be to your liking? It is most probable, you know, in view of what you have told me, that Miss Wayburn is illegitimate."

"As to that, it makes no difference to me," said Jervase simply. "It is my grandfather who is concerned. Since he has been very good to me—and, indeed, unexpectedly sympathetic in what must seem to him sheer madness on my part—I owe it to him to find out what I can. But if Miss Wayburn will accept me, I shall marry her whatever her parentage."

"May I repeat that statement to my client?"

"You may tell him all that has passed between us," confirmed Jervase. "And you will earn my gratitude by doing it as soon as possible. At the moment Miss Wayburn has no notion of my feelings towards her, a state of affairs that I am anxious to remedy without loss of time. Nor do I anticipate an easy conquest," he added ruefully. "The lady is of a very independent disposition. I do not know that she would care a great deal for the stain of illegitimacy—she has accepted it with fortitude for years—but she has an exaggerated reverence for the house of Wrelf. Ranks it far higher, I fear, than that of Guelph! My best hope is to prove to her that the blood in her veins is fit to mate with mine. I might then be able to win her consent."

Mr. Whitehead looked distinctly incredulous. "Surely she must realise the honour you do her? It is the suggestion of such a match for her—if I may so far presume, such a very advantageous match—that gives me some hope of persuading my client to speak."

"And indeed I hope it may succeed. But it will do me no service with his daughter—for I presume he *is* her father, this mysterious client of yours?" He glanced up enquiringly, but the lawyer's expression was perfectly non-committal.

"I will use my utmost powers of persuasion," he promised, "and make what speed I may. But I do not foresee any possibility of securing the information for a week at least. And I must warn you again not to be too hopeful of the outcome. A secret that been guarded for fifteen years is not lightly disclosed."

Lord Stapleford groaned. "A week! Then I shall go back to the Place and await the issue with what patience I may. Another week of idling here would drive me insane. And you will send to me the moment you have news?" And Mr. Whitehead's smile and firm hand clasp confirmed his promise that his new client should not be kept in suspense a moment longer than was absolutely necessary.

On leaving the lawyer's office Jervase weighed
the choice between leaving at once for Stapleford,
which would mean an overnight stop at Basing-
stoke, and the alternative course of setting out at
first light next day which should bring him home
by nightfall. The first course was the more
sensible. The second would permit him time to call
in Bond Street where he had selected a charming
bonbonnière in Chelsea ware, a gift which he felt
that he might, with perfect propriety, bestow upon
Lissa. He had been on the point of concluding its
purchase on the previous day when two of his
friends had strolled into the shop and he had
hastily asked the proprietor to put it aside for him
and made pretence of being deeply engrossed in
selecting a snuff-box. He had already endured
sufficient roasting over his unexplained dalliance
in the wilds of Wiltshire.

He now set out purposefully in the direction of
Bond Street, only to be halted within sight of his
goal by recognition of a lady coming out of the
library. Surely that was the Comtesse de Valmeuse
whom he had left in charge of the schoolroom at
the Place? He crossed the street, her bow and smile
assuring him that his eyes had not deceived him.

He enquired politely how she went on in
London, offering his services if he could be of use to
her in any way. This she gracefully declined,
saying that, her business in Town being happily
concluded, she planned to set out for Stapleford
next day. She added that his little sister had taken
joyously to London life and was already quite

attached to her Goldsborough cousins. He stared
and she realised that he had not been aware of his
sister's presence in Town. The explanation that
followed left him thoroughly uneasy. Certainly it
was the Marquis's right to direct Mary's movements, but when they had talked together there
had been no mention of any visit to these maternal
relatives. Yet no sooner was he safely out of the
way than Mary had been set to packing her trunks.
And why had Lissa been left behind? The Viscount
was no fool and past experience had shown that
his grandfather was entirely without scruples
where the interest of Wrelf was concerned. There
was a grim set to his jaw and a hint of pallor about
the tight-pressed lips.

"You will forgive me, Madame," he said curtly.
"I ride tonight for Stapleford. I am anxious for
Lissa. Oh, no!" for she had paled perceptibly. "Not
for her physical safety. My grandfather would not
harm her. But I was trusting enough to inform him
of my wish to make her my wife, and I would not
put it past him to have contrived her disappearance during my absence—or even, so to have
worked upon her feelings that she might hide
herself away where I could never find her. What a
fool! What a blind, crass fool, to think that he
would so easily accept—But I waste time. Only tell
me your direction and my chaise shall be at your
disposal for your journey tomorrow. For myself, I
leave at once."

Chapter 15

"SHE HAS been gone for five days with no more than a few paltry coins in her purse—and you have no idea where she may be."

The tone was impersonal, certainly not vindictive—and the Marquis felt like a murderer. He had scarcely recognised his grandson when the boy had ridden in at dawn, grey-faced with fatigue and grimed from head to heel with the dust of the roads. There had been no word of apology for his unceremonious irruption into his grandfather's bedchamber at five o'clock in the morning, or for his filthy condition. He simply demanded to know the details of Lissa's going, for the sleepy groom who had stabled his exhausted mount had acquainted him with the bald fact of her disappearance. And the Marquis had nothing to tell him.

He had been miserably uneasy himself since the child had gone. If only she had taken the money he might have been at peace. As it was he stood self-convicted of having cast an innocent girl penniless upon the world. He could not forgive himself—far less expect Jervase to forgive him.

In fact the Viscount was not concerned with
blame or forgiveness. He had listened with fierce
concentration while the Marquis set forth with
complete honesty the account of his dealings with
Lissa, and had spoken only once. When the
Marquis had handed him the note that she had left
he read it through slowly, as though to extract the
last shred of evidence that it offered, his eyes
unnaturally bright in that grey mask of a face.
Then he picked up the packet of money and broke it
open. Several guineas fell and rolled unheeded on
the floor. He unfolded two fifty-pound bills.
"Generous," he said softly.

The Marquis took the blow without flinching. "I
did what I thought right and made adequate
provision," he said steadily, a statement of fact
rather than an apology.

"And when you found her gone?"

"There could be no hiding it. I enquired at the
Vicarage and Mrs. Hetherston undertook to question Mrs. Wayburn. She, too, had received a note.
The girl bade her not to be anxious for she had
taken refuge with friends."

"And you accepted that?"

"I enquired who the friends might be. So far as is
known the child had no acquaintances outside the
village."

The Viscount began to pace slowly up and down
the room, his step heavy and springless with the
fatigue of his night-long ride. The Marquis rang
for his valet and demanded brandy and hot coffee.

"And then?" said the deadly, weary monotone.

The Marquis shrugged. "What could I do? To enquire further was to provoke the very scandal I had been at pains to avoid."

The heavy pacing was resumed. The Marquis poured brandy into a glass and proffered it. It was ignored.

"There are only two people I can think of," said his lordship. "She may have gone to Miss Parminter in London. Heaven send that that be so. But there is also the Hetherston boy. A long-standing childhood friendship there, and a marked degree of attachment. What word of him?"

The Marquis stared. "*That* young whipper-snapper? Hetherston's nephew? No! Never tell me *he's* in the petticoat line. Besides he was away. Staying with friends—where was it, now? West-bury? No; Warminster. And devilish put about, by all accounts, when he heard the girl had gone off like that. Said she must have been the victim of odious persecution to have served us such a trick. Infernal impudence!" But the voice lacked its former masterful ring.

"Then I am for London again. Miss Parminter is my last hope."

"For God's sake, boy! It will do the girl no good if you kill yourself. Here—" He pushed his grandson roughly into a chair—"Drink this." He had added a generous measure of brandy to the hot coffee and Jervase drank it mechanically. The Marquis refilled the cup.

"Get you to bed, lad. Since nothing else will serve, I'll go myself. It's not a business to be entrusted to underlings, however discreet." Then, with a hint of appeal, "For the girl's sake, as well as ours, the less noise the better."

Jervase nodded wearily. He was too spent to think clearly and the brandy was having its effect. "You'll bring her back?"

The Marquis answered the question that had not been put into words. "Yes. No trickery. You have my word. If I can trace her I will bring her back."

It did not occur to either of them that Lissa might refuse to come. Nor did they dwell on the horrid possibility that she might not, after all, be safe under Miss Parminter's wing. While the Marquis made rapid preparations for his journey, Jervase forced his weary mind to concentrate on reporting his interview with the lawyer, though now it seemed distant and unimportant, set against his new anxiety.

It was noon before he woke from the heavy sleep into which he had fallen as soon as he had yielded the initiative to his grandfather, woke to another period of anxious waiting with no prospect of action to relieve the strain. The Marquis should reach Town by evening and he would send word back as soon as there was news, though it was not to be expected that he himself would attempt the return journey immediately, however successful his mission. So two more days at least must pass before he could hope to see Lissa safely home again, and in its present bereft state that home seemed to him no better than a mausoleum. He would go and see Hetherston, the only man who was fully acquainted with all the circumstances.

At least he could then enjoy the privilege of speaking freely.

But Mr. Hetherston had been called to a sick parishioner and only his wife and nephew were at home. He accepted the lady's invitation to take tea with them, hoping that her husband would not be long delayed, but the atmosphere was far from comfortable. In Mrs. Hetherston's enquiries for news of Lissa there was a note of reproach which he resented. He really could not be expected to go around assuring all his acquaintance that his intentions were strictly honourable. Christopher Whitehead had been a different matter, a man of good understanding and one with whom he was unlikely to come in contact save in the way of business. Briefly he explained the present position. Mrs. Hetherston looked relieved and agreed that it was very likely that Lissa had fled to Miss Parminter. Jervase turned thankfully to young Ned, asking his opinion of the matched greys that he had chosen to drive that afternoon. The choice had been deliberate. Though perfectly well-mannered the greys were high spirited and gave their handler no time to indulge in gloomy reflections. Ned was generous with his admiration. His private opinion of Lord Stapleford could not affect his judgement of such a splendid pair and an invitation to try them out went some way towards suggesting that his lordship might not be such a bad fellow as Ned had first imagined. Certainly he had seemed genuinely concerned for Lissa's safety.

By the time that he had tooled the curricle about

the lanes for an hour and had enjoyed an animated
discussion with its owner on the finer points of
driving a pair, a tandem and a four-in-hand, he
was fast coming round to the belief that he had
misjudged his lordship on first acquaintance and
that he was, in fact, a capital fellow. It then
occurred to him that if this was indeed the case he
was doing the capital fellow a great disservice by
concealing Lissa's whereabouts and causing him
a degree of anxiety quite disproportionate to the
true state of affairs. But he had given his word to
Lissa. He fell into uneasy silence, then mumbled
that perhaps his uncle might be returned by now,
and drove very soberly home. His lordship, too
preoccupied to pay more than courtesy attention to
his young companion, thought him a lad of odd
moods. Doubtless he would grow out of them.

Since the Vicar was not yet back there was
nothing for it but to drive home to the prospect of a
long solitary evening. But he had scarcely seen the
greys properly bestowed when there were sounds
of a fresh arrival in the stable yard.

He strode out eagerly, even though reason told
him it could not possibly be Lissa, and was amazed
to see that it was his own light travelling chaise
that was being wheeled into the coach house. Yes,
they had set out from London only yesterday, the
lads told him, and had lain overnight at Brook-
wood. The Comtesse had sent for them less than an
hour after his own departure and had seemed in an
uncommon hurry. His lordship, in a fresh surge of
apprehension, for what could have caused this
unexpected start, made his way to the house.

The Comtesse was just coming downstairs as he entered. She had taken off her hat but had not yet changed her travelling dress and she looked so white and ill that he exclaimed upon it and took her arm to support her to a chair.

"It is nothing," she said faintly. "I am always queazy when travelling. But I *had* to know—" She broke off, seemed to make an effort to gather her forces, and then, ignoring the chair that he had pulled forward, clasped his sleeve and looked up anxiously into his face. "Mrs. Graham tells me that Lissa left this house a week ago and that no one knows where she has gone. I beg of you, my lord, where is the child?"

Only the truth would serve. He told it as gently as possible. "My grandfather has gone in search of her, Madame. We hope that she has sought shelter with Miss Parminter in London."

The Comtesse looked dazed. She put a wavering hand to her head, said vaguely, "But Miss Parminter is not—" and crumpled in a dead faint at his feet.

Chapter 16

THE WEEKS that followed held a nightmare quality that Jervase, in after years, preferred to forget. There being no doctor resident in the village, they began with a breakneck ride into Wilton to summon one, for, in falling, Madame had struck her head against the corner of a heavy oak bench and now lay deeply unconscious. However, on examining his patient, the doctor's report was reassuring. The lady might not recover her senses for several hours and when she did come round her memory of the events immediately preceding her fall might be a little hazy, but there was no cause for alarm. The servants had told him that she had taken nothing but a cup of coffee on the long and tiring journey from Town and doubtless it was the lack of proper nourishment that had caused her to faint, for apart from the blow on the head he could find nothing much amiss with her.

But this relief only freed Jervase to swell with increasing uneasiness on the Comtesse's remarks. The more he thought of it the odder it seemed th she should have been so desperately anxious for Lissa, unless she suspected him of having abducted the girl and hidden her away. And those last words before she fainted—"But Miss Parminter is not—" Not what? Not the safe and suitable refuge that they had imagined? But that was *too* ridiculous. He had known her for years and a more honest and upright woman did not walk the earth. He was allowing his own anxiety to delude him into foolish fancies. Best give up the puzzle and trust that the Comtesse would be sufficiently recovered by morning to explain herself.

But she was still unconscious when an exhausted groom limped stiffly into the library next morning with a billet from his grandfather. The news was the worst possible. The Marquis had gone immediately to General Carnforth's house, only to find it closed—the windows shuttered, the knocker off the door. Moreover no one seemed to know his present whereabouts. Because of his long illness it was months since he had been seen at his club, and being, as the Marquis succinctly expressed it, "such a cantankerous old curmudgeon," he was not on such terms with his neighbors as to encourage intimate knowledge of his movements. The Marquis proposed to make further enquiries, but in the meanwhile he suggested that his grandson should check on any passengers who had joined vehicles passing within walking distance of Stapleford at the vital time. Surely someone would recall seeing the child?

Jervase entered upon this assignment with fierce energy and a hopeful uplifting of his spirit. It

sive figure. Short in stature, lightly built, bow-legged, he looked, in well worn riding dress, more like an ostler or a post boy than an official of the law. He later confided to the Viscount that these were roles that he had frequently played. "And werry 'andy, too, me lord, for the picking hup of hinformation, 'specially if it's aught to do wiv the 'gentlemen of the road' as folks calls 'em."

But the small blue eyes were remarkably shrewd, the brain behind them both keen and methodical. Though he shook his head sadly over the length of time that had elapsed before his expert services had been called in, he was not without hope. Moreover he was pleased to approve such measures as had already been taken. Before leaving Town he had consulted with the Watch and was prepared to give an exact date for the closing of General Carnforth's house. Since this was four days before Lissa's disappearance he thought there was little good to be got by further enquiry in London. "Hif so be as young Miss 'as joined up wiv the party, we'll most likely find 'em in one o' these 'ere spaws wot the nobs goes to when they're out o' frame. And seein' as they're the nearest to 'and, we'll start wiv Barf and Chelt'n'am.

The Viscount objected that he had already checked every possible vehicle which might conceivably have carried Lissa to either of these destinations.

"Yers, me lord. But maybe the old codger—begging yer pardon, Sir—picked 'er up by previous arrangement. Or if that's not the way of it, by wot

you wos a-saying of, you wos asking for a young
lady wiv red 'air. But 'air can be dyed—or it can be
'id under a close bonnet."

Remembering the sad tale of Bertha Williams,
Lord Stapleford realised that there might be a good
deal to be said for this idea, and raised no further
objections.

"Nah, leavin' aside the red 'air, will yer lordship
favour me wiv a full description of the young
party? Or better still—" his eyes ran appraisingly
over the serried ranks of family portraits arrayed
on the walls—"'save yer such a fing as a picsher of
'er?"

The Marquis shook his head regretfully. Jervase
said suddenly, "Yes, Sir, there is. If I can but find
it. Though I don't know if it was ever completed, so
it may not be of much use to us," and took the stairs
to the schoolroom in leaping strides.

He was a little diffident about searching among
such of the Comtesse's possessions as she had left
there without first seeking her permission, but she
was still not fully recovered from the effects of her
fall and kept her bed, puzzling the doctor considerably by the state of dreamy lethargy into which
she had fallen, for which he could find no apparent
cause. Jervase decided that it was better not to
disturb her if he could avoid it. The schoolroom
looked unnaturally bare and tidy, but stacked in a
corner were several portfolios holding sketches.
Almost at once he found what he was seeking.
What was more, the portrait *had* been finished,
and with a loving attention to detail which must,
he felt, prove invaluable. He hesitated no more.

was unfortunate that there was so wide a choice of practicable routes, but remembering Lissa's conspicuous hair he, too, was convinced that she could not have escaped notice. By the end of a week, having extended his original "walking distance" from two miles to six and added carriers' carts and farm tumbrils to the Mails and stage coaches with which he had begun, he had reached two firm conclusions. Unless all the people he had talked with went round with their eyes shut, Lissa had either left the neighbourhood in a private vehicle or she was still concealed somewhere close at hand. Since the first possibility gave rise to such horrid speculations as there was no enduring, he next embarked on a protracted search of any building that might conceivably shelter a fugitive, only to draw a complete blank. Lissa seemed to have vanished as completely as though she had been spirited away.

At this juncture the Marquis came back from London, a tired and anxious man, showing for once the burden of his years. An enquiry at a livery stable that General Carnforth occasionally patronised had elicited the information that there had been some mention of the old man's going to Harrogate—or maybe it was Bath or Cheltenham—the fellow couldn't be sure—but one of those places where sick folk *could* go, so they were sufficiently well breeched.

The Marquis had promptly sought out General Carnforth's physician with the object of discovering which of the popular spas had been favoured with his patient's patronage, only to be told that the doctor had gone on holiday—to Edinburgh, of all outlandish places, announced his housekeeper severely—to study the work of some other medical man. No, she didn't know where Doctor Mansfield was staying. But he would be back in mid-August, because Lady—well, one of his patients, was expecting to be confined about then.

By the time that the Marquis had reached the end of this sorry tale, Jervase was more in sympathy with him than he had been since Lissa's going. Both of them seemed to have spent the time chasing phantoms, both were weary and anxious.

"What did you do then, Sir?"

"I went to Bow Street," said the Marquis simply.

He said it as though it was a perfectly natural and commonplace action for the head of the house of Wrelf to go to Bow Street and submit his private problems to the eye of officialdom. Nothing could have so convinced Jervase of his grandfather's sincerity. Indeed, from no other lips would he have accepted the truth of that simple statement.

"Were they helpful?" he asked, awkwardly, shyly, not knowing how to express his sense of the enormity of the sacrifice.

Lord Wrelf shrugged. "They did their best. They suggested that as no crime appeared to be involved I should engage the services of a man who used to be a Runner but who now undertakes private enquiry work. He will be here tomorrow. One or two points he wanted to follow up in Town, the fellow said, or I'd have brought him down with me."

Mr. Smithers was not, at first sight, an impres-

Chapter 17

"YOU MUST see, my lord, that I cannot possibly tell you where she is," said Miss Parminter firmly. "It would be a breach of trust and unforgivable. She is well, she is in good hands and she is usefully employed. I am sorry for it that you should have been in such anxiety for her, but she *did* leave a message assuring her Stapleford friends of her safety."

"And I am more grateful for your care of her than I can easily say," returned Jervase earnestly. "But I *must* see her. It is relief inexpressible to know that she is safe but I cannot let matters rest at that. My grandfather is already aware of my wish to make Lissa my wife, if she will so far honour me. Since you stand, at the moment, in place of Lissa's natural guardians, it is only proper that you, too, should be informed of my intentions."

To say that Miss Parminter's composure was quite shattered by this announcement is an understatement. Her mouth dropped open, her eyes seemed like to pop out of her head and she fell, rather than seated herself, on the couch that was fortunately conveniently placed. But presently, the first shock assimilated, she sat up straight as was her wont.

"You are serious, my lord? Yes. Of course you are. One does not make jest of such matters. But will the Marquis consent?"

"He has not done so yet. But he has softened amazingly during the past weeks and I am in hopes that he will eventually reconcile himself to the idea."

"But Lissa said—my Lord Wrelf himself informed her—that you were on the point of announcing your betrothal," said Miss Parminter perplexedly.

Jervase's mouth hardened to an inflexible line and then, as the humour of the situation suddenly struck him, relaxed to a grin of pure mischief. "When my grandfather made that statement it was wholly untrue," he said coolly. "And since I cannot have the head of my family convicted of lying, I must obviously do my utmost to turn it into truth as swiftly as I may. Please, Miss Parminter," he coaxed.

But despite her amazement and delight at the sudden turn in Lissa's fortunes, she refused to be persuaded. "I will write to her this very day," she assured him mendaciously, "and I will tell her that I feel it is only right and fair that she should grant you an interview." And I will buy her that muslin gown, she thought grimly, whether she is pleased or not. She is not going to receive his lordship in that old brown thing. Aloud she said politely, "Are you staying in Bath, my lord, or shall I send a message to Stapleford Place?"

"In Bath, at the Pelican in Walcot Street," said his lordship. And seeing her glance of mild surprise that he should choose so modest a hostelry, added, "Neither my grandfather nor I have any cause to be proud of this affair. But it is not only for our own sakes that we wish to brush through it as quietly as possible."

Miss Parminter nodded sympathetically. "Very well, my lord. I will do as I have promised and I wish you a happy outcome."

With that he had to content himself. But he was too restless to remain quietly in the Pelican, whither he had repaired on leaving Gay Street. He was not in the mood for riding and the greys had done enough for one day. He spared a sympathetic thought for Mr. Smithers, no doubt still dutifully pounding Cheltenham-wards. Mr. Smithers had deserved well of him. The advice he had given had led the Viscount without a check to the house in Gay Street. He decided to add a substantial douceur to the fee that they had agreed.

Thankfully he put off his driving coat and buckskins. The Pelican might not lay claim to fashionable preeminence but it gave good service. Careful hands had unpacked his valise, someone had taken pains to press the creases from his coat—the olive green broadcloth that his man had evidently considered indispensable when visiting the Metropolis of the West—while a boy appeared immediately to help him off with his boots and to bring hot water for his ablutions. He stretched himself luxuriously, mind and body at ease for the first time in weeks, and wondered whimsically how many miles he had ridden and driven in pursuit of his elusive love. So they brought him safe to the haven he sought, he would not begrudge them.

Nevertheless this evening he would walk. He pulled on the buff coloured pantaloons, arranged a fresh neckcloth with swift precision and shrugged himself into the coat, settling its high, folded collar carefully and reflecting thankfully that modern fashions were infinitely more comfortable and sensible than the stiff brocades and velvets of his grandfather's day. The fact that these were still de rigeur in Court circles seemed to him an added inducement to abjure Town life.

Out of doors the sun was still warm and the streets seemed stuffy. Instinctively he headed for the promise of coolness beside the river and sauntered casually over the Pulteney Bridge and into Laura Place. Eased of his heavy burden of anxiety he was in the mood to pay attention to his surroundings and noted with interest the way in which the city was growing. Great Pulteney Street was new to him, and he admired its spacious layout which permitted the light breeze to refresh the weary pedestrian. Almost before he was aware of it he was approaching Sydney Gardens and idle curiosity tempted him to go inside. Great plans were afoot to extend the entertainment offered in the gardens to include many of the attractions that Vauxhall and Ranelagh offered to Londoners.

Some of the work was already completed, and though he was a little past the age of succumbing to the temptations of the labyrinth, he enjoyed listening to the gurgles of merriment and the squeals of mock fright emitted by a party of youngsters who were obviously thrilled to the core by its hazards.

They were nearing the exit for their voices were plainly audible. He heard a girlish voice implore, "Oh! Pray let us go round once more! I'm sure I have the secret of it now. We'll be very quick."

He did not catch the low toned answer, evidently a denial, for now a second voice joined in the argument, a childish pipe with a hint of tears not far away as it proclaimed indignantly, "It's not my fault that I have to go to bed earlier than you! 'Tisn't fair to say I spoil all your fun. 'Specially when it's *my* birthday treat and *my* money that paid for us to come in!"

That was certainly a strong case, thought Jervase, amused, and listening with interest to hear how authority would deal with a delicate situation. At this point the leading members of the party emerged from the maze—a couple of school-girls in their early teens and so alike that they must surely be sisters if not twins. Jervase, still eavesdropping shamelessly, heard a new voice say gently, "Don't cry, Susan. You mustn't cry on your birthday, sweetheart, or you'll cry all year."

He sprang forward. The voice was familiar and dear. Had he not spent many pleasant hours in training its cadences? With a heart that, contrary to all the laws of anatomy, seemed to be beating in

his throat and half choking him, he approached
the entrance to the maze. The attendant looked up
hopefully, scenting fresh custom, but Jervase was
oblivious of everything but the slender brown-clad
girl who was leading the still rather watery-eyed
Susan by the hand. Her face was hidden from him
as she stooped over the child but the old-fashioned
bonnet could not disguise Lissa from her lover's
eyes. When she did not even glance in his direction,
intent on comforting her small charge, he swept off
his curly brimmed beaver, bowed and said softly,
"Good evening, Miss Wayburn."

The next moment the hat was cast aside and he
had caught the long-sought fugitive in his arms,
for at the sound of his voice she had lifted to his a
face of such incredulous joy that there could be no
doubt as to her feelings. That first hard kiss was
pressed on lips innocent but warmly responsive.
After which, regardless of the highly interested
twins and the deeply shocked attendant, Lord
Stapleford proceeded to assuage a hunger that had
been six months a-growing within him. Not
realising that the girl in his arms was half dazed
by the sudden revelation of his desire and the fierce
sweep of emotion that his caresses had aroused
within her, aware only that she was pliant and
submissive in his hold, he kissed the childish brow,
the smooth eyelids, the fascinating spot 'twixt
cheek and chin where sometimes a dimple quivered and so came again to her mouth. At which
point a stern voice announced in his ear, "Sir, if
you don't leave off at once I'll call the Watch. Right

down indecent, it is. In broad daylight, too, and in front of those innocent childer!"

Instead of slinking away shamefaced at this reproof, the culprit only glanced up, still keeping one arm firmly round the girl's shoulders as though he feared she might run away, smiled pleasantly and said—cool as you please, as the attendant later told his wife—"You must forgive me, my good fellow, but my betrothed and I have been long parted," and stretched out an appealing hand. Since the hand chanced to contain a couple of guineas the guardian of the moral sanctity of the Sydney Gardens was appeased and the little party was permitted to withdraw in good order.

Lissa, recovering now from the first rapturous shock, withdrew herself gently but decidedly from the shelter of his lordship's arm. "We must make haste," she said. "Miss Meredith will be displeased if we are late. She said seven o'clock, you know, and it would be a pity if she were to forbid our picnic tomorrow."

"Yes," contributed the Viscount briskly. "Run on ahead, girls, and wait for us by the entrance. I want to speak privately with Miss Wayburn."

The twins, already sufficiently female to be susceptible to masculine good looks, especially when allied to a delightful smile and the air of a fellow conspirator, ran off obediently. And if Susan might have preferred to linger she was given no opportunity to do so, her sisters each seizing a hand and bearing her off willy-nilly.

"And now, my little love," said Lord Stapleford gently, "will you not tell me all about it? Why did you feel that you must run away? I have been seeking you everywhere—and my grandfather was in such straits that he called in Bow Street."

"He called in the Bow Street Runners to find *me*?" exclaimed Lissa, incredulous and horrified. "But why? He wanted me to go away so that you could marry the girl of your choice without a scandal. So why should he trouble himself to find me again?"

"Perhaps because I convinced him that *you* are the lady of my choice," suggested his lordship, "though he was also deeply concerned for your safety."

But Lissa was herself again. "No, my lord," she said bluntly. "I am no wife for you as well you do know. It's of no use pretending I don't love you after the way I let you kiss me—" and glorious colour flared under the delicate skin at the memory—"but that was because you took me unawares and it makes no difference. I can't marry you." And she hastened her steps to catch up with the children.

Jervase had half expected this rebuff and since it was prefaced by so frank an avowal of love was not unduly depressed by it. Indeed, he felt that he was in a fair way to attaining his heart's desire. It was just a matter of coaxing and wooing—and what a pleasure that would be—and Lissa would eventually yield. Without undue conceit he could not help knowing that all her friends would add their persuasions to his. Even if he were disinherited—and in his present buoyant mood he felt quite hopeful of bringing his grandfather to

give his consent—he might still be considered a
good match for a penniless governess. Certainly
Miss Parminter had seemed to be of that opinion.

Lissa held other views. Worldly advancement
did not enter into them. Jervase was a
Wyncaster—the heir of Wrelf—and as far removed
from her humble workaday world as a visitor from
Olympus. Lord Wrelf might have failed in his
measures to dispose of her tidily but he had
succeeded to admiration in convincing her that
association with Lissa Wayburn, base-born waif,
spelled ruin for his lordship. She would have none
of him.

She positively refused to return to Stapleford.
She could support herself by her own efforts. And,
since he insisted, despite all her protestations, on
escorting her home, he should see for himself what
a very respectable post she had found. Nor did
Miss Meredith prove the stout ally that he had
hoped. A swift glance at his card had certainly
disposed her in his favour, and his apologies for
having delayed Miss Wayburn and her charges
were graciously received. The stern reprimand
that she had prepared for them was forgotten and
the girls were dismissed to their supper with no
more than an admonition to make haste. But the
suggestion that Miss Wayburn should return to
Stapleford Place was less welcome. While by no
means so besotted about the girl as was her friend
Edith, she acknowledged Lissa's good qualities
and found her services, just at this juncture, both
useful and economical. The Miller girls had taken
a fancy to her and gave no trouble—a marked

change of demeanour—and any replacement would ask at least double the pittance that Lissa had accepted. While sorry to disoblige his lordship she did not feel that she could release Miss Wayburn without due notice given. She was vastly surprised to learn that Lissa did not wish to give notice. That caused her to unbend considerably. She even suggested that perhaps at the end of the month—for surely Miss Beaton would be recovered by then—Miss Wayburn might return to Stapleford for a short holiday.

His lordship then exerted himself to charm her into consenting to the outrageous proposal that he should form a member of the projected picnic party, blandly announcing that he had taken a great fancy to her lively charges and would value an opportunity of improving his acquaintance with them. But this was going too far for Miss Meredith's sense of propriety until he hit upon the happy notion of inviting Miss Parminter to join the expedition. Since neither protagonist consulted Lissa's wishes this was agreed between them and his lordship went off to engage Miss Parminter's support. Lissa, torn between the longing for a whole day spent in his society and the shrinking from its cost in further heartache, pleaded a migraine and went early to bed.

Chapter 18

ONLY THE Miller girls regarded the picnic as an unqualified success. Lissa, though looking charmingly young and biddable in the muslin dress of Miss Parminter's providing, refused to discuss any but the most impersonal topics. When Jervase tried to draw her a little aside from the others she stayed the closer to Miss Parminter's side. There should be no repetition of yesterday's caresses if Lissa could help it. She recognised too well her own weakness in the face of *that* form of persuasion.

So Lord Stapleford found himself charged with the entertainment of three schoolgirls, a fate which he undoubtedly merited in view of his brazen remarks to their preceptress. And though he did in truth, find them likeable and entertaining, this had scarcely been his primary object in joining the expedition.

Lissa, meanwhile, was subjected to a long homily from Miss Parminter. That good friend urged her to consider well before she rejected all that his lordship offered. While in part agreeing

with the girl's view that so unequal a match was a
hazardous business, she would not go so far as to
say that it was inevitably doomed to disaster, or
that his lordship might some day come to regret
his present rashness. Since Lissa remained ob-
durate she spoke next of gratitude and duty. Lissa
had been shown great kindness by the Wyncasters, yet she had left their roof in a clandestine
manner which had caused them considerable
trouble and anxiety. Only to think of Lord Wrelf's
actually going to Bow Street, all to find one
naughty girl! If she persisted in refusing the
Viscount's offer of marriage then the least she
could do was to accede to his request that she
return, however briefly, to the Place. So the world
might see that she had not been driven out by
persecution but had left of her own choice.

To Lissa's reproachful eyes at this defection she
hardened her heart. Lord Stapleford should have
every chance that *she* could win for him, however
low she sank in Lissa's esteem. To see her darling
Viscountess Stapleford she was perfectly willing
to throw overboard the principles of a lifetime. It
was not, she told herself, as though his Lordship
was a rake or a waster. He would make the most
delightful husband.

What was more to the point she was prepared to
offer practical help. When Lissa objected that Miss
Meredith could not spare her, Miss Parminter
promptly countered with an offer to take charge of
the Miller children until Miss Beaton returned to
duty. Her uncle no longer needed her attendance,

Lady Mary was in London, and she would be happy to oblige her future partner. The girls looked rueful. They were inclined to like Miss Parminter who was not near so fusty as most governesses. But she could not compare with Lissa who had been playmate as well as guardian. The three bright faces so woefully clouded touched Jervase's ready sympathy.

"Perhaps your parents would allow you to come to Stapleford for a visit on your next holiday," he consoled.

"Will Lissa be there?" demanded Susan suspiciously.

"That I can't promise," he said, "though I hope very much that she will. You must help me to persuade her."

Lissa felt that she was being pushed into an impossible position—as though it was not already hard enough to do what she felt was right.

"Since you are all so set on it," she said with dignity, "I will consent to return to the Place for a little while. Beyond that I promise nothing."

The children were jubilant. Susan hugged her warmly and Pamela said that she would write to Papa that very night. Miss Parminter pronounced judicially that her decision was the right one. Lord Stapleford, very sensibly, said nothing at all. He had never been one to push his luck too far. It was left to Miss Parminter to suggest that since the weather was so genial it would be very pleasant if he took Lissa up in his curricle. It would be perfectly proper. An open carriage was quite a different proposition from a private chaise. And since there was no reason for delay, why not tomorrow while the good weather held?

To this, too, Lissa assented, with an air of indifference and a tilt to her chin that augured ill for the progress of his lordship's wooing. She might and did adore him—but she had red hair and a mind to match and no liking at all for the subtle sort of blackmail to which she had been subjected.

For the first part of the journey she managed to nurture these feelings of outrage. His lordship might as well have been driving a waxwork figure modelled by Madame Marie Tussaud for all the response he won from her. But there was too much to tempt her to enjoyment. The day was so balmy, the air so sweet with the fragrance of honeysuckle and new-cut hay. The greys, fresh after their day's idleness, buckled to their task with a will, but the curricle was so beautifully balanced and sprung that the pace was exhilarating rather than frightening. With so much to tempt her Lissa could not for ever resist the insidious call of youth and freedom. Why not pretend that all was as fair as it seemed? That she was some high-born maiden driving in company with her betrothed husband with only the stolid Tom perched up behind to play propriety. And when they stopped to rest the horses and Jervase, reaching up his hands to help her alight, said suddenly, "You do not know what happiness it is to have you safe beside me. For today it is enough that you should be alive and well and content to trust yourself to my care. I know that you have been persuaded against your wish but I promise not to tease you with further importunities," there could be no resisting the warm sincerity in face and voice. She smiled back at him, all her love in her eyes, and allowed all thought of anything but present joy to fall away.

They reached Stapleford half-way through the afternoon. As Tom sprang down and went to the horses' heads, Jervase looked down for a moment at his companion, grinned cheerfully and said, "And now to face the dragon! And what an ungrateful wretch I am to describe him so! Frightened?"

"I don't *think* so," said Lissa cautiously. "He has always been very kind to me. But that was before I ran away."

Anti-climax followed. There was no ordeal to face. The Marquis was gone—and Lissa's portrait with him. "Left only an hour or two after your lordship's self," said Humphreys, Lord Wrelf's valet, still indignant that he had been left behind. "Travelling north, I apprehend, and driving himself in the phaeton."

"The phaeton?" said Jervase, blinking. "For a journey north? Which horses?"

"The chestnuts, milord," said Humphreys reverentially, for though *he* was an indoor man the fame of those four matched chestnuts was part of the Wrelf tradition.

Jervase could only imagine that his grandfather had suddenly run mad. There was no close relative whose imminent decease could explain such a crazy start. It seemed most probable,

especially in view of his having taken the picture
with him, that his departure was occasioned by his
partial recognition of its background. But a man
approaching his seventies—and driving a phaeton
and four!

These were sentiments that he could scarcely
express to Humphreys. Instead he enquired how
Madame did. Humphreys cast down his eyes. "I
understand from Mrs. Graham that she is up and
about but keeps to her own room," he said sedately.
"The physician, it appears, is now of the opinion
that some great trouble—possibly the terrible fate
of the late Comte—is oppressing her mind so that it
does not recover its normal tone."

Humphreys, with his precision and his pedan-
try, usually amused the Viscount. On this occasion
he found no cause to smile. He had conceived a
mild liking for the Comtesse and was sorry to hear
so wretched an account of her health. He was more
concerned for Lissa, since he had reckoned on her
being strictly chaperoned, and now, with his
grandfather also away, the position was far from
satisfactory. However a simple solution offered.
He would beg hospitality for himself at the
Vicarage.

This he presently did and was warmly welcomed, especially by young Ned, heartily relieved
that no guilty secret need now mar a promising
friendship. He offered to give up his room—the
best guest chamber—for Lord Stapleford's comfort, gratifying his aunt by such proper behaviour
even though the offer was promptly refused. He
then escorted the honoured guest to a much

smaller room which was pronounced to be very
snug and comfortable, and took the opportunity of
offering frank apology for his deception.

"Turning me up sweet, eh?" grinned Jervase,
cuffing him lightly over the head. "No wonder you
were so magnanimous about giving up your room,
letting me chase round every damned coaching
office in the county hunting for a girl whom you
had quietly lifted away from under my nose. How
you must have smiled to see me so completely
taken at fault!"

"I did at first," admitted Ned honestly. "But
that was before I realised that I had the wrong sow
by the ear. And by then it was too late. I'd promised
Liz, you see, and I couldn't let her down."

"Of course you couldn't. I must have done the
same myself."

"She's a great gun is Liz," amplified her friend.
"We've been good chums ever since she planted me
a facer for calling her 'Coppernob,' the first time
we met." He grinned reminiscently. Then added, in
more serious vein, "True as steel. She'd never let a
chap down."

"If you could only convince her of that," said
Jervase dryly, "you would be doing me a service. I
might even find it in me to forgive you for the trick
you served me." And seeing Ned's mystified
expression, explained, "So far as I can gather, her
only reason for refusing to marry me is the fear
that by doing so she *would* be letting me down."

Ned was a little startled at this frank confidence. Uneasy, too, since he could think of no word
of comfort or advice. He fidgeted miserably about

the room, uncertain whether to stay or to go.
Seeing his distress, Jervase took pity on him and
said briskly, "However, don't imagine you're
going scot-free, Master Impudence. Come up to the
Place tomorrow morning and we'll have the foils
out. *I*'ll teach you a proper respect for your elders,
see if I don't."

Chapter 19

THERE WAS, in fact, time and to spare for several such lessons. They were much in each other's company, fencing, riding and driving about the quiet lanes. Sometimes Lissa joined them, but she spent a good deal of time in the Comtesse's room and so managed affairs that she was never alone with Jervase. He enjoyed young Hetherston's society but found himself waiting with growing impatience for news of his grandfather or from Mr. Whitehead.

Lissa's return seemed to have put new heart into the Comtesse. When first the girl went in to visit her, the invalid had held out frail white hands and drawn her close to be clasped and kissed with a fervent, "Dieu merci! You are safe!" and Lissa had felt the soft cheek pressed against hers wet with tears. But though they spent long hours in each other's company they spoke little, Lissa busying herself with embroidery, the Comtesse gazing out in the summer glory of the gardens but so lost in her own thoughts that it was plain she did not see them.

Once, when Lissa sighed over sorrowful thoughts of her own, the Comtesse reached out and touched her wrist, murmuring, "Do not grieve, child, nor be anxious. It will end well, I promise you," and Lissa found the confidence in the quiet voice oddly reassuring.

On Thursday morning the Comtesse announced her intention of coming downstairs. She was much stronger, her mind seemed perfectly clear, and she was, she explained, expecting a visitor. This gentleman was coming from London and should arrive in the early afternoon. If convenient she would like to receive him in the library. A little surprised at this punctilious formality, Jervase gave good natured assent.

"And I would like both you and Lissa to be present at the interview," went on the Comtesse, "though I would be obliged if you would permit us the privilege of five minutes' private talk first."

This seemed puzzling but probably had some simple explanation. Jervase thought it likely that he and Lissa were to be invited to witness the Comtesse's signature to some legal document and dismissed the matter from his mind. He wondered once more how soon he might hope to have word of his grandfather. He was beginning to suffer some anxiety on that head. It was unlike the old man to have sent no word of his activities.

He had intended to drive into Warminster that afternoon with Ned and Lissa to meet the friends who had aided the escape, but the expedition must now wait until Madame's business was done. He suggested that they should adjourn to the billiard room. He and Ned could have a hundred up and perhaps Lissa, who did not play, would consent to mark for them. So he did not see the arrival of Madame's visitor and when, presently, a footman announced that Madame la Comtesse would be pleased if they would join her in the library, it was with a sense of severe shock that he found himself shaking hands with Mr. Christopher Whitehead.

"I will not, for the moment, present you to the lady," said the Comtesse, with a tight little smile in Mr. Whitehead's direction. "Lord Stapleford you know already. He will be interested to learn that I am the 'client' who can help him to clear up the mystery in which he is interested."

Mr. Whitehead bowed. "That is correct, my lord," he said gravely. "You will recall that I informed you that I had received no answer to my letter. The delay was caused by Madame's illness."

None of this seemed quite real to Jervase. The suddenness with which it had burst upon him gave the scene the quality of a dream. Gravely he returned Mr. Whitehead's bow and awaited further revelations. The Comtesse, as though her brief flare of energy was already spent, sank into a chair. Lissa, bewildered by a conversation which meant nothing to her, ran to Madame's side and asked if she should bring some restorative.

"No," said the Comtesse abruptly. "And perhaps, in a moment or two, you will not wish to be doing me that service. Mr. Whitehead will explain."

In the billiard room, Ned Hetherston, after playing one or two desultory shots, replaced the

cues in their rack and wandered over to the
window, hoping that his friends would not be too
long. He was thus privileged to observe the arrival
of the most dashing equipage that it had ever been
his good fortune to see. So absorbed was he in the
perfection of the matched chestnuts drawing the
phaeton that he paid no heed at all to its occupant.

Mr. Whitehead cleared his throat and wondered
how best to go about his difficult task. He looked at
the Comtesse, her face resigned to a calm acceptance of what must come, yet strangely vulnerable,
and he was touched to compassion.

"In what follows," he said firmly, "let me make
it perfectly clear that the facts which I am about to
reveal would, in any case, have been made public
very shortly. Lord Stapleford's intervention has
only accelerated their disclosure."

The Comtesse gave an infinitesimal shrug. The
man was loyal and kindly disposed, but—n'im-
porte!

"When the Comtesse de Valmeuse visited my
office recently," continued Mr. Whitehead, "she
rehearsed to me a full conf—er—account of the
facts concerning the child known as Lizzie Wayburn."

"Confession will do, Mr. Whitehead," inter-
posed the Comtesse dryly.

Mr. Whitehead blushed. "This account proves
beyond doubt that the child in question is, in
fact—"

"The Lady Alicia Kentsmere," said another
voice from the library doorway, "only child of

Robert, twelfth Baron Kentsmere and his wife, Angela."

The little group that had been listening so closely to Mr. Whitehead that they had not marked the opening of the door, swung round to stare at the newcomer. The Marquis of Wrelf came in composedly, stripping off his driving gloves, as though the delivery of such thunderbolts as the one that he had just launched was mere commonplace. The Comtesse, who had been prepared for just this revelation, though not, perhaps, in quite such bald phrases, was the first to recover.

"Your information, my lord Marquis, is perfectly correct. Had I realised the extent of your knowledge I might have spared Mr. Whitehead a wearisome journey."

"My knowledge, Madame, was the merest supposition, until you so obligingly confirmed it," said the Marquis, grim-faced. "I could think of no other explanation that fitted the facts."

"But what *are* the facts?" demanded Jervase.

The Marquis's grim visage relaxed. Almost, he smiled. "Told you I knew that house, boy. Found it right away. There's a sketch of that very frontage in the guide book. Kentsmere House. That's where I've been, this past sennight, and heard a queer garbled tale from every gossip in the place. Even the children have it by heart, though it's fifteen years old. So then I went to the parsonage to get the truth. And when I showed the old fellow the painting—" he set the Comtesse's portrait of Lissa on the mantel shelf—"he said at once that it was a likeness of the Lady Angela in her girlhood. His verion of the story was more restrained than the others I had heard, but shocking enough for all that."

He turned to Lissa, who was listening, white-faced, stealing occasional glances at the Comtesse, who, since the Marquis's arrival, had never once glanced her way. "Come here, child," he said gently.

She went to him slowly. He took her face between his hands and went on, "You have been an orphan since you were three years old. Your parents died together when the yacht in which they were crossing from France was lost with all hands. You were left to the guardianship of your aunt—Madame la Comtesse, here—" and the harsh note was back in his voice as the fierce old eyes turned again to the Comtesse. "Of what followed immediately I have no knowledge, save that within the year the child, Alicia Kentsmere was lost. The village had several versions; stolen by gypsies—drowned in the river that fed the mere—these were the most credible. At about the same time the child, Lizzie Wayburn, answering in every particular to the description of the missing Alicia Kentsmere, was brought to Stapleford by Mr. Jonathan Whitehead. No doubt the Comtesse could fill in the details for us."

The Comtesse glanced at Mr. Whitehead and nodded. "You may read that part of my statement which describes these events," she said quietly. "But first I would have you understand that Mr. Jonathan Whitehead was no party to the fraud. He

thought the child was mine—an indiscretion that I
would fain hide before I sailed for France—and
marriage."

The lawyer sighed his relief and unfolded the
document that he had all this time been holding.
He turned over a page or two and then read on.

"From the time of my sister's marriage I had
lived alone at Storey Court. Upon her death I did
not change my domicile but I formed the habit of
driving over to Kentsmere House several times a
week to ensure that all was well with my niece. On
this occasion I entered the grounds by the South
Lodge which had stood empty for some months, so
that no one knew of my presence. I had driven only
a little way when I caught sight of the child herself
playing, apparently unattended, on the river bank.
That is very dangerous, I thought. Alicia saw me
and came scampering up to the gig, bubbling with
laughter because 'Nurse had fallen asleep.' I went
over to the woman to rebuke her for her careless-
ness, and saw at a glance that she was dead. It was
later stated at the coroner's enquiry that she had
died of an apoplexy. I did not want the child to be
frightened so I suggested that she should come
with me for a turn about the grounds. It was after I
had lifted her into the gig that the sudden
temptation came. If I could carry her off, unseen as
I had come, then her heritage would pass to
me—and I could marry Gilles. If I chanced to be
seen, then no harm was done. My actions could be
easily explained."

Mr. Whitehead turned the page. The Marquis
said, "So simply done. And in the confusion that

arose when the nurse's body was discovered, it was some time before the child was missed. Everyone assumed that she was in the care of some other member of the household. But it defeats the imagination. That a woman, gently bred and close kin to that pathetic scrap, should so succumb to the lure of gold."

The Comtesse's tragic eyes looked him over dispassionately. There was a touch of disdain in the curl of her lip. "You would not understand," she said. "The child will—even if she cannot bring herself to forgive. She loves your grandson as I loved Gilles. Do you think I wanted her fortune for its own sake? I wanted only to be Gilles's wife. I, a Protestant, and near penniless—he, scion of one of France's oldest Catholic families. And poor. Desperately poor. His parents would not hear of marriage between us. And in France it is the parents who decide."

She fell silent a moment, thinking of what was past. "I paid," she went on wearily. "Do not think that I escaped unpunished. Gilles never knew of my crime, but always in my heart there was the guilt, the remorse. My lord Marquis deems me a monster of iniquity. But I had been fond of the child—and I dare not even provide for her as befitted one of gentle birth. Had she been placed with people of quality there must have been more enquiry into her antecedents—as indeed happened. And then I, too, had a child. A son, tawny haired, like Alicia. He died when he was four—at much the same age that—" She pressed a clenched fist against quivering lips, but went on almost

immediately, "I knew then that full payment
would be exacted, but still I would do nothing that
might harm Gilles. And then he, too, was taken
from me—and so terribly." She shivered. "Well—it
is done now. I have made what amends I can. I
strove to escape the final punishment—that I
should bring dishonour on the name I bear—
Gilles's beloved name. But it was not permitted.
Even I—" she rounded on the Marquis—"steeped
in infamy as you think me, would not rob these
children of their chance of happiness. So it is all set
down—and you may do with me as you will." She
raised one hand slightly, indicating the document
in Mr. Whitehead's grasp, then folded both in her
lap, her face closed, impassive, awaiting their
judgement.

The Marquis cleared his throat in embarrassment. Damn the woman! Guilty as hell—and yet
she touched even him to pity. Jervase's eyes were
soft with it. Though he grieved for Lissa's lost
girlhood, yet it would be his delight to make up for
the stolen years. And dimly he perceived how the
Comtesse's desperate action had started the chain
of events that had brought them to the present
moment. She had sent Lissa to Stapleford. Today
she had given Lissa to him as surely as though she
had given her in marriage.

There came a soft rush of muslin skirts and
Lissa was kneeling beside the Comtesse's chair,
her warm young hands clasped over the fragile
cold ones.

"They shall not, Madame," she said simply.
"They shall not dishonour his name. I will not

permit it. It is for *me* to say. And I do, indeed, understand. Tempted as you were I might well have yielded as you did, if it had been for my lord. As it stands now you have given me back my name and the right to marry where I love."

She rose, a glory of happiness in her face as she held out both hands to Jervase, though still in voice and bearing was the note of determination, gentle but inflexible. "My lord, if it is still your wish, I may come to you with an honourable name and a love that matches yours. Will you choose to take me, as I am, or will you rather choose to punish a sin that has been more than atoned?"

It was only a stride for Jervase to reach her. He dropped on one knee and kissed her hand. "My lady," he said softly, "*your* honour is mine. As you will soon bear my name, so I will pay due tribute to yours. No slur, however remote, shall fall upon it. What has passed within this room shall be forgotten."

He swung to his feet, eyes challenging his grandfather to argument. Lissa's hand still clasped in his.

"Very sensible, my boy, very sensible," said the Marquis gruffly. "Bygones—eh?"

Mr. Whitehead heaved a great sigh of relief and bent over the Comtesse, offering his arm to help her to her feet and support her from the room. The Marquis crossed swiftly to open the door for her and, as she passed, dropped one hand on her shoulder in a pressure that left blue finger-bruises for nigh on a week. Lissa was held close in his lordship's arms. He said, "A month, my child. No more. I have waited too long already. Besides if we wait longer the holiday will be at an end—and you must have those Miller brats for your bridesmaidens. It was they, after all, who restored my little lost love to my keeping."